CHALDEAN CHRONICLES

WEAM NAMOU

HERMiZ
PUBLiSHING

Library of Congress Cataloging-in-Publication Data
2025919296

Namou, Weam
Chaldean Chronicles
(Nonfiction)

ISBN
978-1-945371-20-2 (paperback)
978-1-945371-21-9 (eBook)

First Edition

Published in the United States of America by:
Hermiz Publishing, Inc.
Sterling Heights, MI

10   9   8   7   6   5   4   3   2   1

CONTENTS

Introduction vii

1: Who Are the Chaldeans? 1

2: Abraham's Lineage and the Chaldeans 5

3: Biblical and Early Christian Perspectives on the Chaldeans 8

4: First Mention in Archaeology (9th Century BCE) 11

5: The Chaldean Tribes and the Nimrud Letters (9th–7th Centuries BCE) 14

6: The Assyrian Deportation of the Chaldeans (9th to 7th Century BCE) 16

7: Chaldo's Rebellion and Chaldean Resistance (7th Century BCE) 18

8: The Chaldean Account of Genesis (19th Century CE Research) 20

9: Berossus: The Chaldean Priest of Babylon (3rd Century BCE) 24

10: Sibyl, the Chaldean Prophetess (2nd Century BCE) 26

11: Chaldean Rulers in Northern Mesopotamia (7th–6th Century BCE) 28

12: Nebuchadnezzar II: The King of Kings (6th Century BCE) 31

13: Lives of the Judean Exiles in Babylon (6th Century BCE) 33

14: The Chaldeans in Jewish Thought: Talmud and Kabbalah (3rd–13th Century CE) 35

15: The Fall of the Chaldean Empire (6th Century BCE) 37

16: The Babylonian Astronomical Diaries (7th to 1st Century BCE) 39

17: Greek Chronicles of the Chaldeans: Anabasis and Beyond (5th–2nd Century BCE) 41

18: Naburimannu, a Chaldean Astronomer and Mathematician (6th–3rd Century BCE) 44

19: Kidinnu, Astronomer and Scholar (4th Century BCE) 47

20: Sudines, Astronomer and Mathematician (4th Century BCE) 49

21: Seleucus of Seleucia (2nd Century BCE) 51

22: The Influence of Chaldean Sciences on Greek and Roman Scholars 53

23: Church of the East (1st Century AD) 58

24: Julian the Chaldean (2nd Century CE) 60

25: Chaldeans and Christianity in China, 400 AD 62

26: Saint Hirmiz Chaldean Church (397 AD) 63

27: Nestorius: The Controversial Archbishop of Constantinople (5th Century AD) 65

28: The Chaldeans and the Adoption of Nestorianism 67

29: Discovery of the Chaldean Lost Scrolls 71

30: Chaldean Christianity in Abbasid Babylonia (9th–10th Century CE) 73

31: Chonain, the Nestorian Christian (9th Century CE) 75

32: Ibn Wahshiyyah: A 10th-Century Muslim Scientist, Alchemist, Translator 78

33: Early Medieval Christian Rule (10th–11th Century CE) 81

34: Michael the Great (1199) 82

35: Sabrisho ibn al-Masihi (1226-1257 AD) 85

36: Chaldeans in Medieval Pisa (12th–13th Centuries CE) 87

37: Yahballaha III (1281–1317 AD) 88

38: The Little Book on the Knowledge of the World and the Chaldeans in Mesopotamia (1404) 90

39: 1457 World Map.. 92
40: The Legacy and Marginalization of the Chaldeans............................. 93
41: Persecution and the Loss of Chaldean Heritage 96
42: The 1445 Cyprus Union with the Vatican... 99
43: Patriarchate of Yohannan Sulaqa (1551).. 100
44: Pietro della Valle and Sitti Maani (17th Century) 102
45: Nation of the Chaldeans (1617) 107
46: The Scribes and Writers of Chaldean Heritage 108
47: Josephus Adjutus (17th Century Chaldean Scholar)......................... 112
48: Elias al-Musili, First Middle Easterner to Travel to the Americas (17th Century)115
49: Alqosh—A Chaldean Town and the Tomb of the Prophet Nahum 118
50: Maria Theresa Asmar: Author and Traveler (19th Century).............. 120
51: Hormuzd Rassam: Archaeologist and Diplomatic Pioneer (1826-1910) 123
52: Rev. Joseph Naayem: Priest, Scholar, and Humanitarian (1868 – 1964) 127
53: The Modern Assyrian Identity 129
54: Evidence of the Chaldean Presence in Modern and Historical Contexts......... 134
55: The Chaldean Language: A Legacy of Aramaic 138
56: DNA Testing 141
57: The Thrones and Palaces of Babylon and Nineveh (1876)................... 145
58: Chaldeans in Argentina.. 148
59: Chaldeans in India 150
60: Rediscovery of Chaldean Heritage... 153
61: A Chaldean in Afghanistan.. 155
Epilogue 158
Notes 163
Image and Illustration References... 185

CHALDEAN CHRONICLES

INTRODUCTION

"Chaldeans, hold on to your ethnicity. Trust the testimony of your own books and ancestors over Western sources, all day, every day."

—Father Augustine, Nineveh-Chaldean monk
(Manuscript from 1880)

Over two decades ago, while working at my computer, I came across the Wikipedia page for Telkaif. To my surprise, the town—long known as Chaldean—was suddenly labeled as Assyrian. How could such a change happen so easily? Growing up, I had always known Telkaif as Chaldean, a fact deeply rooted in family stories, books, and cultural traditions. In 2000, I visited the town, stayed with my relatives, and enjoyed its natural beauty—from fresh dairy breakfasts prepared by Bedouin women to picnics by waterfalls and visits to ancient monasteries. Everyone I met there, including Muslims, spoke of the town as Chaldean.

As I looked closer, I discovered that Wikipedia's open-edit platform allows anyone to alter information. While this fosters knowledge-sharing, it also opens the door to inaccuracies and deliberate distortions. It amazed me how easily history could be rewritten by those with an agenda.

Throughout history, people have manipulated narratives to serve political purposes, and Wikipedia is no exception. After 2001, a coordinated effort began to replace the term "Chaldean" with "Assyrian" in key historical definitions. When outright substitution proved difficult, editors adopted a subtler approach: "Chaldeans are ethnically Assyrian but belong to the Chaldean Catholic Church."

This argument leans on the claim that "Chaldean" is not an ethnicity but a term introduced in the 16th century. Yet if Chaldeans were not a distinct people, why would the Vatican use this name? Why did so many notable figures identify as Chaldean long before that era? And where is the proof that Chaldeans are ethnically Assyrian?

Determined to find answers, I researched for years and discovered that Chaldeans are their own ethnicity, with their own language and their own history. We are Chaldeans, and we are Catholic. Our faith is not our ethnicity. So, where has this inaccurate blending of Chaldeans with Assyrians—one that has caused great harm among our Aramaic-speaking communities—come from?

I soon discovered a troubling pattern: a coordinated group of editors has monopolized Wikipedia entries to replace the Chaldean identity with that of the Assyrian. When others attempt to correct these edits, they are often blocked, and the misinformation persists. A notable case is the Wikipedia page titled "Chaldean Catholics," which was repeatedly vandalized and merged with the "Chaldean Catholic Church" page. By viewing the "Talk" section, one can trace the extensive efforts to overwrite this identity.

Historically, erasing a group's identity required war or violence; today, it is achieved digitally—what is now called Information Warfare. Similar disputes have affected other Middle Eastern groups defending their histories online, including Syriac Arameans and Kurdish Jews.

Of course, one might say that, as a Chaldean, there's bias in my perspective—just as every writer brings their history and perspective to the page. But intent matters. Those who seek the truth rely on evidence and welcome critique. That's why I opened myself to debates on X (formerly Twitter) to find any missing links in my research. Despite heated exchanges and personal attacks, no one produced a single verifiable source proving that Chaldeans are ethnically Assyrian.

My search for answers deepened as I became the Executive Director of the Chaldean Cultural Center in Michigan, home to the world's only Chaldean Museum. There, I found undeniable evidence of the continuous existence of the Chaldean people, documented by historians, travelers, and scholars through the ages. I also discovered that the modern Assyrian identity remains a topic of debate, with some scholars suggesting that the groups once referred to as "Nestorians" were historically Chaldean.

So, are we the same people? In certain respects—geography, language, and faith—we share deep roots and overlapping histories. But that does not erase our distinctions. Calls to merge Chaldeans and Assyrians under a single name often claim to promote unity, yet unity cannot come from erasure. If someone told you that the man you've known as your father isn't your father, would you simply accept it without evidence? You'd seek the proof. And if none was provided, being told, "What does it matter—both men are from the same town," wouldn't resolve the truth of your own identity. Likewise, our community seeks understanding, not substitution.

For a people officially recognized in Iraq but often

misunderstood abroad, preserving the Chaldean identity is not an act of division—it is an act of loyalty. Honoring our heritage affirms the resilience of our ancestors and gives purpose to the generations who will follow. As other ancient peoples, such as Native Americans, have done, we, too, safeguard our culture out of love and moral responsibility toward those who came before us.

Through *Chaldean Chronicles*, I aim to reclaim and celebrate that enduring legacy. Structured in concise, evidence-based chapters, this work serves as both a historical record and a tribute—offering readers a deeper appreciation of the Chaldean people's remarkable story.

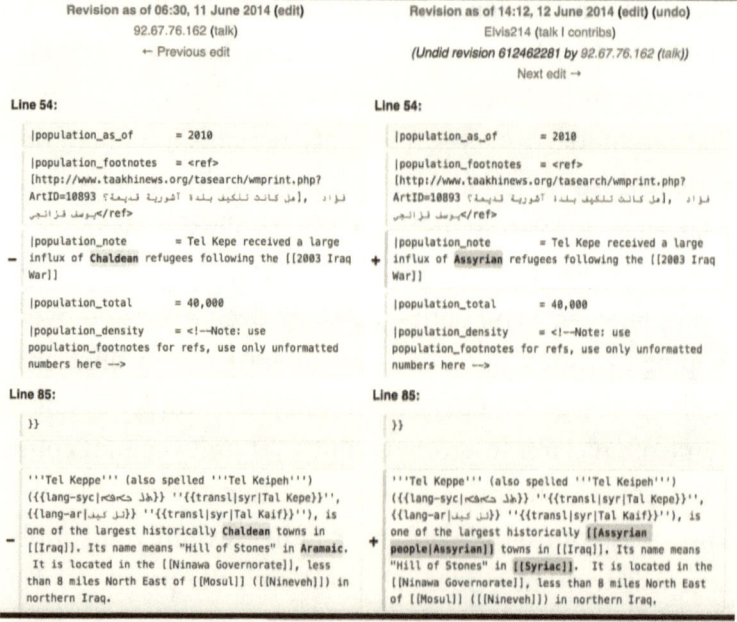

Image of Wikipedia edit history of *Telkaif*, where "Chaldean" was replaced with "Assyrian" in describing the town and people. This example illustrates how online editing can reshape collective memory and redefine ethnic identity in the digital age.

ENTRY 1

WHO ARE THE CHALDEANS?

Chaldean Origins in Mesopotamia

The Chaldeans of Mesopotamia—modernday Iraq, eastern Syria, and southeastern Turkey—are part of the region's ancient heritage. Their history dates back over 5,000 years (some historians claim 7,000 years), making *Chaldeans* one of the oldest terms still in use. Known in Aramaic as *Beth Nahrain*, or "the land of the two rivers," Mesopotamia was the fertile cradle of the Tigris and Euphrates. This land became home to some of the world's earliest civilizations, including the Sumerians, Akkadians, Babylonians, and Aramaeans—peoples from whom the Chaldeans trace their origins. Many scholars describe "Chaldean" as an umbrella term uniting these ancient Mesopotamian ethnicities.

Mesopotamia, derived from the Greek for "land between rivers," was the birthplace of transformative cultures. It was here that humanity first established the foundations of writing, law, and science. As Rhonda Byrne writes in *The Secret*:

> The ancient Babylonians and their great prosperity have been well documented by scholars. They are also known for creating one of the Seven Wonders of the World, the Hanging Gardens of Babylon.

Through their understanding and application of the laws of the Universe, they became one of the wealthiest races in history.

This region's legacy of innovation and cultural achievement continues to shape how we view human progress today.

Connection to Ur of the Chaldeans and NeoAramaic

Chaldeans trace their roots to *Ur of the Chaldeans*, the birthplace of the Prophet Abraham. They speak NeoAramaic—the language of Jesus Christ—which was historically called *Chaldean*. As rulers of the NeoBabylonian Empire, they were not only military strategists but also intellectual pioneers. Under their leadership, Babylon became a beacon of enlightenment, celebrated for its advancements in science, culture, and governance.

Scientific, Cultural, and Political Contributions

The Chaldeans excelled in astronomy, creating detailed star catalogs and introducing the sexagesimal (base-60) numerical system that still underpins modern timekeeping and geometry. Babylon's libraries preserved and expanded knowledge in medicine, law, and mythology, building upon earlier Sumerian and Akkadian traditions.

The Russian noblewoman and philosopher Helen Petrovna Blavatsky once wrote:

> The ancients were always distinguished—especially the Chaldean astrologers and Magians—for their ardent love and pursuit of knowledge in every branch

2

of science. They tried to penetrate the secrets of nature in the same way as our modern naturalists, and by the only method by which this object can be obtained, namely: by experimental researches and reason. If our modern philosophers cannot apprehend the fact that they penetrated deeper than themselves into the mysteries of the universe, this does not constitute a valid reason why the credit of possessing this knowledge should be denied them or the imputation of superstition laid at their door.

Blavatsky's words remind us that the Chaldeans were not merely ancient stargazers but true scientists of their time—using reason and observation to uncover the mysteries of the universe.

Religion and Cosmology

Religious practices among the Chaldeans centered on deities like Marduk and reflected a cosmology that linked human existence with celestial phenomena. This intellectual and spiritual environment profoundly shaped the experiences of the Judean exiles, leaving a lasting imprint on their cultural and religious development.

Resilience Through the Ages

For thousands of years, the Chaldeans have faced immense challenges, including oppression, genocides, and relentless attempts to erase their name and heritage. Yet through their resilience, spiritual strength, and rich intellectual legacy, they have not only survived but preserved their unique identity and culture.

As we move through the entries ahead, we'll explore how the Chaldeans—often overlooked in history books—profoundly influenced the ancient world and carried their legacy into modern times. Let's begin by examining their portrayal in biblical and early Christian texts.

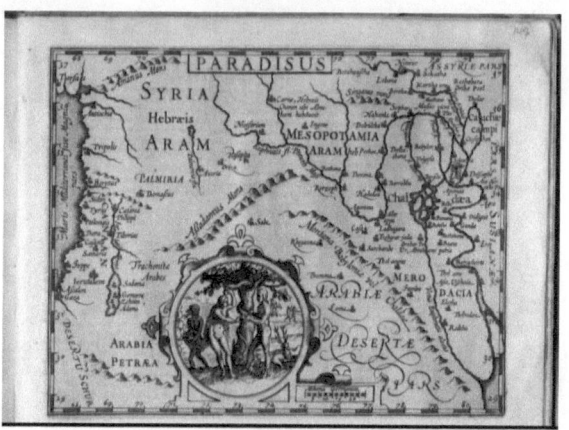

Map from 1607 showing the Holy Land extending from the Mediterranean Sea to Chaldea (presentday Iraq), reaching the mouth of the Tigris River at the Persian Gulf. The map identifies "Paradise" between the four rivers near Babylon, visually linking scriptural geography with ancient Mesopotamian cosmology. At the bottom, a detailed vignette depicts Adam and Eve beneath the apple tree—symbolically grounding the Chaldean landscape within humanity's earliest sacred narrative.

ENTRY 2

ABRAHAM'S LINEAGE AND THE CHALDEANS

Abraham, often called the "father of nations," is believed to have originated among the ancient Semitic people known as the Chaldeans (referred to as *Calans* in some traditions). He was born and raised in Ur of the Chaldeans (Genesis 11:31), a city located in ancient Mesopotamia, corresponding to modern-day Iraq. This region, historically called the Land of Shinar, was central to the Chaldeans' settlement and is closely tied to their origins as descendants of Shem, the ancestor of all Semitic peoples.

The Descendants of Shem

The biblical genealogy traces Abraham's lineage back to Shem, one of Noah's sons who survived the Great Flood (Genesis 10:22–24).

Shem's key descendants include:

- Arphaxad: Ancestor of the Chaldeans, and through his line, Abraham.
- Aram: Father of the Aramites (or Arameans), who inhabited the region corresponding to modern-day Syria.
- Ashur: Predecessor of the Assyrians, who established a powerful empire centered in northern Mesopotamia.

The first-century Jewish historian Flavius Josephus also highlights this lineage, noting that Arphaxad named the Arphaxadites, "who are now called Chaldeans."

In Genesis, Shem's importance is emphasized through several key moments:

- His role in the flood: When Noah became drunk and lay exposed, Shem and his brother Japheth respectfully covered him.

- His blessing: Because of his respectful actions, Shem received a special blessing from Noah.

- His Messianic Lineage: The biblical genealogy traces the line from Shem, through his son Arphaxad, all the way to Abraham and eventually to Jesus Christ. The *Gospel of Luke* explicitly includes Arphaxad in the lineage of Jesus.

These connections underscore the Chaldeans' place within a broader Semitic framework that shaped the religious and cultural landscape of the ancient Near East.

This photograph captures an archaeological excavation at the ancient Ziggurat of Ur in southern Iraq, led by British archaeologist Sir Leonard Woolley in the 1920s–1930s. The site, known in the Bible as *Ur of the Chaldeans*, reveals the mud-brick ruins of one of the most important Sumerian cities

ENTRY 3

BIBLICAL AND EARLY CHRISTIAN PERSPECTIVES ON THE CHALDEANS

The Israelite View of the Chaldeans

Biblical texts reflect the Israelites' perception of the Chaldeans, often shaped by historical conflicts and cultural contrasts. For example:

- In *Job 1:17*, the Chaldeans are portrayed as raiders who attacked Job's servants and livestock.

- In *Daniel 2:2*, the Chaldeans appear as astrologers and diviners in King Nebuchadnezzar's court.

- In *Isaiah 47:12–13*, they are criticized for their reliance on sorcery and divination:

  "Keep on, then, with your magic spells and with your many sorceries, which you have labored at since childhood.
  Perhaps you will succeed, perhaps you will cause terror. All the counsel you have received has only worn you out!"

Although frequently criticized in the Bible, their spiritual practices were rooted in advanced knowledge of astronomy, mathematics, and metaphysics. What others dismissed as "sorcery" often reflected a profound grasp of the cosmos.

Early Christian Critiques of Chaldean Practices

Early Christian theologians adopted similar critiques, urging converts to reject Chaldean traditions. In the *Doctrine of Addai* (4th–5th century CE), for example: "…and from divinations, and soothsaying, and necromancers, and from fates, and nativities, in which the erring Chaldees boast themselves; and from stars, and the signs of the Zodiac…"

This rejection helped Christianity define a distinct identity apart from older spiritual systems. Yet, viewed in historical context, these texts reveal dialogue, not pure opposition, between emerging Christian theology and Mesopotamian wisdom.

A Nuanced Legacy

Despite negative portrayals in sacred texts, the Chaldeans' contributions to science, mathematics, and mysticism reveal a more complex truth. Babylonian archives unearthed in 2015 show that Israelite captives during the Babylonian Exile enjoyed rights and privileges similar to those of the locals—evidence of coexistence rather than simple domination.

Early Christian Conversion and Mystical Understanding

When St. Thomas the Apostle passed through Mesopotamia on his way to India, the Chaldeans welcomed his message. Their long engagement with metaphysics allowed them to integrate Christian teachings with their own mystical tradition, recognizing continuity between Christ's message and their search for divine wisdom.

Modern Scholarly Reflection

Nineteenthcentury thinkers also noted this continuity. Julius Wellhausen, in *Prolegomena zur Geschichte Israels* (1883), observed: "...everywhere among the writers of the Chaldean period, the close connection is striking in which monotheism is conceived with the unity of worship (Jer. 2:28; 11:13)."

For Wellhausen, the link between divine unity and centralized worship in the Chaldean context helped inspire Israel's own turn toward monotheism.

ENTRY 4

First Mention in Archaeology (9th Century BCE)

Assyrian Inscriptions and the First Records of the Chaldeans

The Chaldeans (Kaldu in Akkadian) first appear in Assyrian inscriptions under Shalmaneser III (858–824 BCE). His annals record: "I went down to Chaldea (and) captured their cities. I received the payment of the kings of Chaldea. Awe of my weapons overwhelmed them as far as the Bitter Sea."

These accounts portray a network of tribal communities inhabiting the marshlands near the Persian Gulf—remote yet strategically positioned between major trade routes.

Chaldean Rivalries and Neo-Assyrian Correspondence

Correspondence from the reigns of TiglathPileser III (745–727 BCE) and Sargon II (722–705 BCE) reveals the intense rivalries among Chaldean leaders such as Mukinzeri and Merodachbaladan. One letter pleads: "Why do you remain inactive while the Chaldean land is getting paralyzed?

Is it pleasing to you that Balassu is giving Chaldea to destruction?"

These exchanges highlight the political volatility of southern Babylonia, where competing loyalties repeatedly drew the attention of empire.

The Chaldeans in the Reign of Esarhaddon

By the time of Esarhaddon (680–669 BCE), the Chaldeans had become an essential part of regional diplomacy. A letter describes Elamite rulers debating whether to interfere in Chaldea to free it from Assyrian domination. Ultimately, the Elamite king refused, saying, "I will not disregard my treaty." This restraint reflects the delicate balance of alliances that defined ancient Near Eastern politics.

Beyond Politics: Cultural Influence

Beyond their political roles, the Chaldeans acted as cultural intermediaries, bridging Babylonian tradition with later Judeo-Christian thought. This influence is explored in George Smith's *The Chaldean Account of Genesis* (1876), which examines how ancient and biblical narratives intersect to shape early theology.

The restored ruins of Ur in modern-day Iraq, identified as *Ur Kaśdim (Ur of the Chaldees)*, traditionally regarded as the birthplace of Abraham. The site features the reconstructed Ziggurat of Ur.

ENTRY 5

THE CHALDEAN TRIBES AND THE NIMRUD LETTERS (9TH–7TH CENTURIES BCE)

The Chaldean tribes, or "houses" (Akkadian: *bītu*), formed five semiindependent principalities controlling southeastern Mesopotamia near the Persian Gulf. The most powerful, BitYakin, ruled the marshy Sealand under MerodachBaladan II, who briefly seized the Babylonian throne—a figure known from both Assyrian records and Hebrew Scripture in *Isaiah* and *2 Kings*.

Other tribes, such as Bit-Dakkuri and BitAmukkani, influenced Babylonian politics, their chiefs occasionally claiming the crown before being defeated by Assyrian forces. Each tribe operated like a small kingdom, laying the groundwork for the later rise of the NeoBabylonian Empire.

Evidence of their activity survives in the Nimrud Letters, a collection of Assyrian royal correspondence from the eighth century BCE. Written during the reign of Tiglath-Pileser III (745–727 BCE), these documents record military campaigns and diplomacy involving various Chaldean leaders. Excavated at Nimrud (ancient Kalhu) and studied by archaeologist Henry W.F. Saggs, the letters reveal that the Chaldeans were organized and politically engaged long before their imperial ascendancy.

This photograph, titled *Constantinople Chaldean* (1869), captures a man dressed in traditional Turkish attire, posed against an ornate backdrop. He is depicted holding a rifle and smoking a pipe, symbolizing aspects of his cultural identity and status. The image was taken by the renowned photographers Abdullah Frères, known for their documentation of the Ottoman Empire and its diverse peoples.

ENTRY 6

THE ASSYRIAN DEPORTATION OF THE CHALDEANS (9TH TO 7TH CENTURY BCE)

Assyrian Control of Babylonia

Before instituting largescale resettlement policies, the Assyrians consolidated control over Babylonia and Chaldean territories. During the reign of TiglathPileser III (r. 745–727 BCE), a Chaldean who had seized Babylon's throne in 728 BCE was deposed—a turning point marking the beginning of centuries of tension between the two powers.

Assyrian Resettlement Policies

Beginning with Ashurdan II (934–912 BCE), the Assyrian Empire implemented a systematic program of relocation to reinforce imperial control. Historian Karen Radner explains:

> People were not made to leave on their own but did so together with their families. They were not snatched away in the heat of battle or conquest but were chosen as the result of a deliberate selection process, often in the aftermath of a war that had very possibly reduced their original home to ruins.

This policy largely targeted urban elites, craftsmen, and scholars, resettling them in Assyrian heartland cities such as Nineveh, Kalhu, and Assur to stimulate cultural and economic growth.

During TiglathPileser's reign, large deportations weakened Chaldean autonomy. His records speak of "hundreds of thousands of Chaldeans" relocated across the empire. His successor, Sargon II (r. 722–705 BCE), continued this strategy to suppress rebellion and consolidate control.

Enduring Identity

Despite repeated displacement, the Chaldeans preserved their heritage and language. By the late seventh century BCE, under Nabopolassar (r. 626–605 BCE), they overthrew Assyrian dominance and established the NeoBabylonian Empire—a testament to their resilience and enduring sense of identity.

ENTRY 7

CHALDO'S REBELLION AND CHALDEAN RESISTANCE (7TH CENTURY BCE)

Babylon Under Assyrian Rule

After the removal of the Babylonian king MerodachBaladan by the Assyrian monarch Esarhaddon, power was divided between the king's two sons. Ashurbanipal governed Assyria, while Shamashshumukin—nicknamed "Chaldo"—was placed on the throne of Babylon.

Though this arrangement appeared to ensure peace, deep resentment lingered among Babylon's priestly and political elite. Many viewed Assyrian dominance as a threat to their cultural identity. Shamashshumukin, despite being Esarhaddon's appointed vassal, sympathized with the Babylonian desire for autonomy and preservation of ancestral traditions.

The Rebellion of Shamashshumukin

In 652 BCE, Shamashshumukin launched a rebellion against his brother Ashurbanipal. This uprising was not merely a struggle for political independence but also an assertion of Babylonian and Chaldean identity. The revolt united numerous allies—Babylonians, Chaldean tribes, Elamites, and discontented neighbors—who rallied to reclaim Babylon's dignity under foreign rule.

Despite early victories, the revolt faltered under the relentless Assyrian siege. By 648 BCE, Ashurbanipal's armies surrounded Babylon, severing its food supply and turning resistance into starvation. Facing inevitable defeat, Shamashshumukin chose death over surrender—setting fire to his own palace and perishing in the flames.

Legacy of Resistance

Shamashshumukin's reign (668–648 BCE) was brief yet symbolically powerful. His rebuilding of temples and public works reflected his commitment to Babylon's spiritual and civic renewal. A monumental relief in the British Museum portrays him carrying a basket of clay on his head, a traditional Mesopotamian gesture symbolizing temple construction and humility before the gods.

Though his rebellion ended in flames, Shamashshumukin's defiance embodied Babylon's enduring spirit. It paved the moral pathway for later insurrections and foreshadowed the Chaldean revival under Nabopolassar in 626 BCE, when the NeoBabylonian Empire reclaimed Mesopotamian independence.

ENTRY 8

The Chaldean Account of Genesis (19th Century CE Research)

Cultural Borrowing and Historical Erasure

Cultural borrowing and historical erasure have shaped civilizations since antiquity, and the legacies of the Chaldeans and Assyrians are no exception. In *The Chaldean Account of Genesis* (1876), George Smith examined creation and flood narratives preserved on Mesopotamian tablets. He demonstrated how Assyria adopted and repurposed the religious and literary traditions of Babylonia and the Chaldeans. Smith observed:

> Although it was known that Assyria borrowed its civilization and written characters from Babylonia, yet, as the Assyrian nation was throughout the greater part of its independent existence hostile to the southern and older kingdom, it could not be guessed beforehand that the peculiar national traditions of Babylonia would have been transported to Assyria.

Smith concluded that Assyrian literature often reproduced Chaldean and Babylonian sources:

> Most, if not all, of them, are, it must be remembered, of Chaldean or Babylonian origin, the Assyrians

having either slavishly copied Babylonian originals or simply put into a new form the story they had borrowed from their southern neighbors.

Corroboration from Other Sources

In *History of Egypt, Chaldea, Syria, Babylonia, and Assyria*, Gaston Maspero agreed with Smith's conclusions, emphasizing Chaldea's primacy in ancient science and art:

> It was from Egypt and Chaldea that the knowledge and the arts of antiquity—astronomy, medicine, geometry, physical and natural sciences—spread to the ancestors of the classic races. Assyria received all her inspirations from Chaldea—her civilization, her manners, the implements of her industries and of agriculture, besides her scientific and religious literature: one thing alone is of native growth, the military tactics of her generals and the excellence of her soldiery.

Maspero observed that Assyria lived only for warfare; when its armies failed, its civilization disintegrated:

> From the day when Assyria first realized her own strength, she lived only for war and rapine; and as soon as the exhaustion of her population rendered success on the field of battle an impossibility, the reason for her very existence vanished, and she passed away.

Together, Smith and Maspero reestablished the Chaldeans as the true intellectual founders of Mesopotamian civilization.

Chronology of Key Moments

- 1. **19th–17th century BCE:** Earliest versions of the Flood story—such as the *Atrahasis Epic*—emerge in southern Mesopotamia, home of the Chaldeans.

- 2. **9th century BCE:** The Chaldeans first appear in Assyrian inscriptions, though their cultural influence predates these records.

- 3. 7th century BCE: The Flood narrative of the *Epic of Gilgamesh* is preserved in Ashurbanipal's library at Nineveh, copied from older Chaldean texts.

Scholars now acknowledge the Chaldeans as both the originators and preservers of many Mesopotamian traditions. Despite Assyrian efforts to obscure their role, Chaldean wisdom endured—reshaping the intellectual heritage of the ancient Near East and beyond.

George Smith

Born: March 26, 1840, London, England

Died: August 19, 1876, Aleppo, Syria (aged 36)

Fields of Study: *Epic of Gilgamesh*, Assyriology, Mesopotamian Archaeology

ENTRY 9

BEROSSUS: THE CHALDEAN PRIEST OF BABYLON (3RD CENTURY BCE)

Life and Historical Context

Berossus, a Chaldean priest of Babylon, wrote during the early Hellenistic period c. 281 BCE. His threevolume *Babyloniaca*, composed in Greek and dedicated to Antiochus I Soter, sought to reconcile the Babylonian past with the Greek present.

Born around 350 BCE under Achaemenid rule, Berossus was trained in temple scholarship devoted to BelMarduk and steeped in Sumerian and Akkadian texts. Fluent in Greek, he became both translator and cultural mediator, correcting Greek misunderstandings about Mesopotamian cosmology.

The Seleucids' focus on Seleucia undermined Babylon's importance, prompting Berossus to preserve his city's heritage through literature. In the preface of his *Babyloniaca*, he identified himself proudly as "a Chaldean priest of Bel."

The Babyloniaca

Babyloniaca was structured into three parts:

1. **Cosmology and Mythology** —Berossus introduced the creation narrative from the *Enuma Elish* and the sage Oannes, a halffish, halfhuman being who brought civilization to humankind.

"Oannes gave men the knowledge of letters and sciences and crafts of all types … and in general provided everything connected with the civilized life." (*FGrH* 680 F 1)

2. **Babylonian History** —Spanning mythical kings like Alorus to historical monarchs such as Nebuchadnezzar II, including the Flood story featuring Xisuthrus (Noah's Babylonian counterpart).

3. **Recent History** —Covering the NeoBabylonian era, its conquest by Persia, and Alexander's entry into Babylon. Berossus emphasized continuity rather than decline.

Legacy and Influence

Through Greek translation, Berossus ensured that Chaldean astronomy, astrology, and mythology entered Hellenistic and Roman thought. Later sources such as Josephus, Eusebius, and Pliny the Elder preserved fragments of his work.

Near the end of his life, Berossus moved to the Greek island of Cos, founding a school of astrology that influenced Hellenistic science. His ability to bridge civilizations cemented his status as the last great priest of Babylon and the first true historian of the Chaldeans.

Berosus Caldaeus

ENTRY 10

SIBYL, THE CHALDEAN PROPHETESS (2ND CENTURY BCE)

Berossus's Era: Babylonian Origins

The Sibyl, called "the Chaldean," was traditionally believed to be the daughter of Berossus. The term *sibulla* in Greek means "prophetess." Her heritage placed her within Babylon's ancient traditions of astronomy, religion, and wisdom.

Flavius Josephus, in *Antiquities of the Jews*, records her prophecy about the Tower of Babel:

> The Sibyl also makes mention of this tower and of the confusion of language when she says thus: "When all men were of one language, some of them built a high tower as if they would ascend to heaven; but the gods sent winds and overthrew it, and gave every one his peculiar language; and for this reason it was that the city was called Babylon."

This oracle linked her Chaldean lineage to scriptural tradition, emphasizing Babylon as a place of divine intervention and universal separation.

Alexander the Great: The Babylonian Warning

In 323 BCE, Babylonian seers reportedly warned Alexander

the Great not to enter Babylon, foretelling his death there. Some sources attribute this prophecy directly to the Chaldean Sibyl. When lexander disregarded the warning, he entered the city and soon fell ill, dying under mysterious circumstances.

Her role in this legend reflects the ancient Chaldeans' reputation for wisdom and astral foresight, blending myth and historical memory in equal measure.

Legacy and Enduring Influence

The Sibyl's oracles were later compiled into the *Sibylline Books*, consulted by Romans in times of crisis. Early Christian writers such as Lactantius saw her as a pagan prophet who prefigured the coming of Christ, bridging Babylonian prophecy with Christian revelation.

Her image endures in Renaissance art, most notably in Michelangelo's Sistine Chapel, where the Chaldean Sibyl occupies a place among the great prophets of the Old Testament, symbolizing the unity of ancient wisdom and divine truth.

ENTRY 11

CHALDEAN RULERS IN NORTHERN MESOPOTAMIA (7TH–6TH CENTURY BCE)

The Rise of the Chaldeans

Long before Christianity emerged, the Chaldeans rose to prominence in the 7th century BCE, emerging as a dominant force in Mesopotamia. From 626 to 539 BCE, they governed much of northern Mesopotamia, marking the final eclipse of Assyrian power. Following the Assyrian collapse, "the Semitic peoples dwelling in the northern lands of Mesopotamia would never gain their independence again," as Babylon assumed control under Nabopolassar and his successors.

Nabopolassar and the Fall of Nineveh

Nabopolassar, a tribal Chaldean leader, led a decisive revolt against Assyria. In 612 BCE, his alliance with the Medes and Scythians brought the fall of Nineveh, the Assyrian capital—a moment immortalized in the *Babylonian Chronicles*. This victory ended centuries of Assyrian dominance and inaugurated the NeoBabylonian Empire—the first resurgence of Babylonian hegemony since the time of Hammurabi.

Consolidation and Cultural Revival

Nabopolassar's reign not only secured Chaldean political power but also sparked a cultural renaissance. Massive reconstruction projects—temple restorations, canal repairs, and fortifications—revived the grandeur of Babylon. By invoking Marduk, Babylon's patron deity, Nabopolassar presented himself as a divinely sanctioned restorer of order and piety. His efforts, especially in rebuilding shrines to Ishtar and Ninurta, set the architectural foundation for the later works of Nebuchadnezzar II.

Travel and Migration

By the first millennium BCE, travel across Mesopotamia was facilitated by improved infrastructure of roads and rivers. Migration to major urban centers such as Nineveh was now far simpler than the long trade expeditions of earlier ages.

Analysis of Major Ancient Journeys Originating from Ur

Journey 1 – Ur → Nineveh

- Approximate Distance: ~805 km (~500 mi)
- Estimated Travel Time: 6–8 weeks
- Primary Terrain / Route Characteristics: Rivers and plains
- Anticipated Challenges: Seasonal floods or political delays

Journey 2 – Ur → Afghanistan

- Approximate Distance: ~2,500 km (~1,550 mi)
- Estimated Travel Time: Several months – 1 year
- Primary Terrain / Route Characteristics: Desert and mountain passes
- Anticipated Challenges: Hostile terrain, banditry, extreme climate

Journey 3 – Ur → Indus Valley

- Approximate Distance: ~3,200 km (~2,000 mi)
- Estimated Travel Time: Several months – 1 year
- Primary Terrain / Route Characteristics: Overland or maritime routes
- Anticipated Challenges: Political instability, logistical complexity

These migrations reflected both the political reorganization of Mesopotamia and the Chaldeans' ability to reestablish urban life and commerce after the wars of the 7th century BCE.

ENTRY 12

Nebuchadnezzar II: The King of Kings (6th Century BCE)

Divine Kingship and Cultural Glory

Nebuchadnezzar II (605–562 BCE), the most renowned of the Chaldean monarchs, transformed Babylon into the intellectual and architectural heart of the ancient Near East. Unlike the Assyrian warlords before him, he defined his reign not merely through conquest but through devotion to the gods and the rebirth of his city.

Nebuchadnezzar styled himself as "King of Babylon, the favorite of Marduk." His inscriptions invoke divine favor and moral humility: "To Marduk, my lord, I make supplication... Guide in a straight path the king whom thou lovest... Create in my heart the worship of your divinity."

Works of Faith and Engineering

Among his greatest achievements were monuments that blended religious symbolism with unparalleled craftsmanship:

- **The Ishtar Gate** — Lined with blue-glazed brick, adorned with lions and dragons representing Ishtar and Marduk.

- **The Processional Way** —A ceremonial avenue for festivals such as the Akitu (New Year) celebration.

- **The Hanging Gardens** —Legendary terraced gardens, reportedly constructed for his Madian queen Amytis.

- **The Etemenanki Ziggurat** —The massive "House of the Foundation of Heaven and Earth," believed to have inspired later accounts of the Tower of Babel.

Spiritual Significance

While Assyrian rulers boasted of military terror, Nebuchadnezzar saw himself as a servant of the divine. His faith forever linked Babylon's political authority with its religious mission.

The biblical tradition enshrined his title "King of Kings" (Daniel 2:37), reflecting his status even among his rivals.

Legacy

Nebuchadnezzar II left a city of temples, palaces, and gardens that embodied the zenith of Chaldean civilization and redefined the ideal of sacred kingship for centuries to follow.

ENTRY 13

LIVES OF THE JUDEAN EXILES IN BABYLON (6TH CENTURY BCE)

Assyrian and Chaldean Policies Compared

The Neo-Assyrians, after seizing Israel (722–721 BCE), controlled subject peoples through forced dispersal and terror. By contrast, Nebuchadnezzar II incorporated exiled Judeans into Babylonian society by granting land and requiring service. As Laurie Pearce notes, "They appear to have been well provided for and did not suffer humiliating treatment."

Economic Integration and Community Life

The Al Yahudu tablets (sixth to fifth centuries BCE) document Judean traders, farmers, and families settled along the Chebar River. Men and women bought land, registered marriages, and engaged in commerce—evidence of a thriving diaspora. Curator Filip Vukosavović remarks: "They weren't slaves; they were residents—and active participants in local business."

Faith in Exile

This prosperity fulfills Jeremiah's directions to the captives: "Build houses and settle down, plant gardens and eat what they produce ... Seek the peace of the city" (Jeremiah 29:5–7).

The Judeans followed these instructions, forging a communal identity rooted in spiritual resilience and adaptation.

Reassessment of Exile

Far from a period of misery alone, the Babylonian exile became a time of cultural exchange and renewed faith, laying the groundwork for Jewish intellectual life in later centuries.

ENTRY 14

The Chaldeans in Jewish Thought: Talmud and Kabbalah (3rd–13th Century CE)

Chaldean Wisdom and Jewish Mysticism

The intellectual legacy of the Chaldeans profoundly influenced Jewish learning after the exile. Renowned for their astrology, dream interpretation, and cosmology, they shaped the development of the Talmud and later the Kabbalah.

Celestial Influences and Dreams in the Talmud

- *Shabbat 156a* attributes temperaments to planetary forces, yet stresses free will—an ethical refinement of Chaldean determinism.
- *Berakhot 55a–56b* treats dreams as "letters that must be read," mirroring Chaldean belief in visions as portals to the divine.

Chaldean Cosmology Reflected in Kabbalistic Texts

The *Sefer Yetzirah* and the *Zohar* echo Chaldean concepts of creation through numerical and linguistic vibration. Even H. P. Blavatsky described Kabbalah as a "Chaldean science of divine numbers."

Shared Themes and Dualities

Both Chaldean and Jewish systems saw light and darkness as interacting principles. Kabbalistic teachings about the *Qliphoth* ("husks") echo Chaldean demonology, while the Talmud prescribes protective prayers and amulets—folk remnants of Babylonian magic.

A Unified Legacy

Through centuries of dialogue and exile, Chaldean astral mysticism merged with Jewish metaphysics. From this fusion emerged the framework for later Christian and Western esotericism.

ENTRY 15

THE FALL OF THE CHALDEAN EMPIRE (6TH CENTURY BCE)

Conquest and Transition

In 539 BCE, Cyrus the Great of Persia captured Babylon, ending Chaldean sovereignty but not its civilization. Rather than annihilation, the conquest ushered in continuity—Chaldean scholars and administrators entered Persian service, sustaining Mesopotamian science and governance.

Legacy Under Foreign Rule

The Achaemenids honored Babylonian traditions, preserving the work of Chaldean astronomers and scribes. This intellectual resilience allowed the Chaldean legacy to endure through the Seleucid, Parthian, and Sassanid eras. As Habib Hanoona writes in *The Chaldean Exodus* (2022):

"The Chaldean nation still exists, and its journey has not been cut off. The claim of its disappearance is false."

Conversion, Faith, and Survival

During the Sassanid period (3rd–4th centuries CE), many Chaldeans converted to Christianity. Under Shapur II, waves of persecution scattered communities across northern Iraq and Anatolia. Later, under Islamic rule, some accepted conversion while others maintained their faith and language through centuries of adversity.

Enduring Heritage

Despite empire after empire, the Chaldeans preserved their name and identity. Their achievements in astronomy, law, architecture, and faith reverberated through antiquity and into the modern age—a civilization that refused to fade.

ENTRY 16

THE BABYLONIAN ASTRONOMICAL DIARIES (7TH TO 1ST CENTURY BCE)

The Babylonian Astronomical Diaries, spanning from the 7th to the 1st century BCE, are among the greatest achievements of ancient science. These cuneiform tablets, discovered in the library of King Ashurbanipal in Nineveh and now housed in the British Museum, document centuries of celestial observations, economic data, and historical events. Compiled by the Chaldean priestscholars of southern Babylonia, the diaries showcase the intellectual depth of their creators and laid the foundation for modern scientific inquiry.

Systematic Celestial Observations

The Chaldeans were renowned as the scientists of their era, adopting a systematic, datadriven approach to understanding the heavens. Unlike speculative horoscopes, their observations of planetary movements, eclipses, and other celestial phenomena were grounded in rigorous methodology. They believed that planetary movements were divine signs, using these patterns to warn rulers of potential dangers. This early use of pattern recognition and predictive modeling marked a significant precursor to the scientific method.

Records of Daily Life and History

Beyond astronomy, the diaries also recorded daily life in Babylon, including weather patterns, market prices, and major historical events. One notable entry documents the death of Alexander the Great in June 323 BCE:

"The king [Alexander] died. Clouds were in the sky. The moon was visible."
(*Astronomical Diaries and Related Texts from Babylonia*, Hunger & Sachs, Vol. III.)

This brief yet poignant record exemplifies the Chaldeans' practice of linking celestial events with significant terrestrial occurrences. Entries like these not only provide modern historians with exact dates for key events but also offer a glimpse into the economic, administrative, and intellectual life of ancient Babylonia.

Enduring Scientific Legacy

The influence of the Chaldeans extended far beyond their time and region. Under Persian and Hellenistic rule, their scientific traditions endured and were integrated into broader intellectual frameworks. Greek scholars such as Hipparchus and Ptolemy drew heavily on Babylonian methods, incorporating them into their own astronomical studies.

The Babylonian Astronomical Diaries remain a testament to the Chaldeans' enduring legacy in science and human history. Their meticulous observations and innovative methodologies bridged the gap between ancient practices and modern scientific inquiry, securing their place as pioneers of astronomical and historical recordkeeping.

ENTRY 17

GREEK CHRONICLES OF THE CHALDEANS: ANABASIS AND BEYOND (5TH–2ND CENTURY BCE)

The term *Anabasis*, meaning "expedition" or "march up" in Greek, appears in the works of two prominent historians: Xenophon and Arrian. Both authors chronicle military campaigns through Mesopotamia and neighboring regions, offering valuable perspectives on the peoples encountered by Greek forces, including the Chaldeans.

Xenophon's Anabasis and the Chaldeans

The Greek soldier and historian Xenophon (c. 430–354 BCE) recorded his famous *Anabasis*, the story of the "March of the Ten Thousand" through Mesopotamia and Armenia after the failed campaign of Cyrus the Younger in 401 BCE. In this account, Xenophon describes encounters with the Chaldeans (Χαλδαῖοι, *Chaldaioi*):

> These troops were Armenian and Mardian and Chaldaean mercenaries belonging to Orontas and Artuchas. The last of the three, the Chaldaeans, were said to be a free and brave set of people. They were armed with long wicker shields and lances. (*Anabasis* IV.3.4–5)

41

Xenophon portrays the Chaldeans as an organized, militarized people living in the mountainous region north of Mesopotamia. He distinguishes them from neighboring Armenians and Assyrians, identifying them as a distinct group. This testimony offers a rare glimpse into the Chaldeans as an active and independent people during the 4th century BCE.

Arrian's *Anabasis of Alexander* and the Chaldeans

Centuries later, Arrian (c. 86–160 CE), a Greek historian and Roman official, wrote his *Anabasis of Alexander*, a detailed account of Alexander the Great's campaigns. Like Xenophon, Arrian's work highlights the Chaldeans' significance. He writes:

> The Chaldeans appear in Hebrew under the name *Casdim*, who seem to have originally dwelt in Carduchia, the northern part of Assyria. The Assyrians transported these rugged mountaineers to the plains of Babylonia. The name of *Casdim*, or Chaldeans, was applied to the inhabitants of Mesopotamia, the Arabian desert near Edom, those who dwelt near the river Chaboras, and the priestly caste who had settled at a very early period in Babylon, as we are informed by Diodorus and Eusebius. Herodotus says that these priests were dedicated to Belos. Inscriptions prove that the ancient language was retained as a learned and religious literature. This is probably what is meant in Daniel 1:4 by "the book and tongue of the Casdim."

Arrian's account, though written centuries after Xenophon's, draws on earlier traditions and emphasizes the Chaldeans' enduring reputation as priests, astrologers, and scientists. His work bridges Greek expeditions and historical understandings of the Chaldeans.

Conclusion

The works of Xenophon and Arrian, though separated by centuries, share a common theme of Greek expeditions into the Near East and encounters with the Chaldeans. Xenophon's firsthand account highlights the Chaldeans as a militarized and distinct people in the mountainous regions of Mesopotamia, while Arrian's *Anabasis of Alexander* reflects their broader historical and cultural significance. Together, these histories provide invaluable insights into the interplay between Greek military campaigns and the enduring legacy of the Chaldeans.

ENTRY 18

NABURIMANNU, A CHALDEAN ASTRONOMER AND MATHEMATICIAN (6TH–3RD CENTURY BCE)

Nabu-ri-man-nu (also spelled Nabu-rimanni; rendered as *Ναβουριανός* in Greek and *Naburianus* in Latin) was a prominent Chaldean astronomer and mathematician who flourished between the 6th and 3rd centuries BCE. His work exemplifies the intellectual achievements of Babylonian science during this period, particularly in astronomy and mathematics.

Mentions in Classical and Cuneiform Sources

Nabu-ri-man-nu's significance is highlighted in both Greek classical texts and Babylonian cuneiform records:

- **Strabo's Geography (16.1.6):** The Greek geographer Strabo of Amaseia describes the Chaldeans as renowned Babylonian philosophers and astronomers with specific settlements in Babylon. He writes:

  In Babylon a settlement is set apart for the local philosophers, the Chaldaeans, as they are called, who are concerned mostly with astronomy; but some of these, who are not approved of by the others, profess to be writers of horoscopes. (There is also a tribe of the Chaldaeans, and a territory inhabited by them, in the neighborhood of the Arabs and of the Persian Gulf, as it is called.) There are also several tribes of the Chaldaean astronomers. For example, some are called Orcheni [those from Uruk], others Borsippeni [those from Borsippa], and several others by different names, as though divided into different sects which hold to various dogmas about the same subjects. And the mathematicians make mention of some of these men; as, for example, Kidenas, Nabourianos, and Soudines.

This reference underscores Nabu-ri-man-nu's inclusion among the most notable Chaldean scholars, alongside Kidenas and Soudines, and highlights the Chaldeans' reputation for astronomical expertise.

- **Cuneiform Colophon (VAT 209)**: A damaged Babylonian clay tablet contains a System A lunar ephemeris for the years 49–48 BCE. The text identifies itself as the *tersitu* of Nabu-[ri]-man-nu. Although the exact meaning of *tersitu* is unclear, scholars speculate it could mean "table," "tool," or even refer to a type of enamel paste. P. Schnabel (1923–1927) suggested that *tersitu* denotes authorship, attributing the development of Babylonian System A for calculating solar and lunar ephemerides to Nabu-ri-man-nu.

Contributions to Astronomy and Mathematics

Nabu-ri-man-nu is credited with pioneering Babylonian System A, a sophisticated method for calculating planetary and lunar ephemerides. This system employs a step-function approach, simpler but highly consistent compared to the zig-zag linear functions of System B. Both systems remained in use until at least the 1st century BCE.

- **Dating System A's Origins:** The earliest preserved System A clay tablets, including BM 36651, 36719, 37032, and 37053, calculate Mercury's ephemeris for the years 424–401 BCE. Lunar tablets from the Hellenistic period date to 306 BCE. These findings suggest that Nabu-ri-man-nu likely lived between the Persian and Macedonian conquests of Babylonia.

- **Calculation of the Synodic Month:** Nabu-ri-man-nu's calculation of the synodic month (the period between successive New Moons) as 29.530614 days is remarkably precise, differing only slightly from the modern value of 29.530596 days. This showcases the exceptional accuracy of Babylonian astronomy and its reliance on detailed observational data.

Legacy

Nabu-ri-man-nu's work represents the pinnacle of Babylonian scientific achievement, combining observational rigor with mathematical innovation. His inclusion in Strabo's *Geography* highlights his enduring reputation among ancient scholars, while his precise calculations, such as the synodic month, demonstrate the advanced state of Babylonian astronomy. The methodologies he helped develop influenced subsequent astronomical traditions, leaving a lasting legacy in the study of the heavens.

ENTRY 19

Kidinnu, Astronomer and Scholar (4th Century BCE)

Kidinnu (also known as Cidenas in Greek sources) was a renowned Chaldean astronomer and mathematician credited with groundbreaking contributions to Babylonian astronomy. He is most famously associated with the "Kidinnu constant," an exceptionally precise calculation of the solar year, reflecting the advanced mathematical and observational expertise of the Chaldeans.

System-B and Innovations in Lunar Astronomy

Kidinnu is believed to have developed System-B, an innovative method for predicting the motion of the Moon, planets, and other celestial bodies. This system accounted for the Moon's varying speed due to its elliptical orbit, employing a step-function model that allowed for highly accurate predictions. Such work exemplifies the Babylonian tradition of meticulous sky observation, combined with arithmetical techniques to model celestial phenomena.

Legacy and Influence

Kidinnu's extraordinary observational skill is evident in his calculation equating 251 synodic months with 269 anomalistic months. This achievement demonstrated a profound understanding of lunar motion and established a foundation for future astronomical studies. His work significantly influenced Greek astronomy, with scholars like Hipparchus and Ptolemy adopting his values for the length of the solar year and the synodic month.

ENTRY 20

SUDINES, ASTRONOMER AND MATHEMATICIAN (4TH CENTURY BCE)

Sudines (or Soudines) was a Chaldean astronomer and mathematician who played a significant role in transmitting Babylonian astronomical knowledge to the Hellenistic world. He is mentioned in Greek and Roman sources, such as Strabo, as one of the prominent Chaldean scholars of his time.

Contributions to Astronomy

Sudines is associated with computations for predicting lunar eclipses. The Roman astrologer Vettius Valens notes: "I thought it best to use Hipparchus for the Sun, Sudines, Kidenas, and Apollonius for the Moon." (*Anthologies* 9.12)

It is believed that Sudines authored tables of lunar data, such as eclipse records, which later informed the work of Greek astronomers. Although his specific writings have not survived, his influence is evident in the methods adopted by figures like Hipparchus and Ptolemy.

Sudines is also credited with providing a particular value for the solar year, though the accuracy of this value remains a subject of debate. Strabo emphasizes his importance alongside other notable Chaldean astronomers, stating: "The mathematicians make mention of some of these men, such as Kidenas, Nabourianos, and Sudines." (*Geographia* 16.1.6)

Influence and Legacy

Sudines is remembered for his pivotal role in bridging Babylonian and Greek astronomical traditions. His work reflects the advanced mathematical and observational techniques of the Chaldeans, as well as their integration of astronomy with astrological practices.

In addition to his astronomical contributions, Sudines is referenced by Pliny the Elder for his observations on gemstones: "Sudines states that in onyx one finds a white band resembling a human fingernail, as well as the color of the 'chrysolith,' the sard, and the iaspis." (*Natural History* 37.24)

ENTRY 21

Seleucus of Seleucia (2nd Century BCE)

Seleucus of Seleucia was a Chaldean astronomer and mathematician celebrated for his support of the heliocentric model initially proposed by Aristarchus of Samos. Born in Seleucia on the Tigris, the capital of the Seleucid Empire, Seleucus exemplifies the integration of Babylonian scientific precision with Hellenistic theoretical advancements. He is also recognized for his pioneering work on tides, which combined detailed Babylonian observations with Greek theoretical frameworks.

Contributions to Astronomy

Seleucus is one of the few ancient astronomers known to explicitly advocate for the heliocentric theory, which posits that the Earth rotates on its axis and revolves around the Sun. According to Plutarch, Seleucus was the first to prove the heliocentric model through reasoning, though the specifics of his arguments remain unknown. Scholars speculate that his reasoning involved mathematical and geometrical methods, building on the rich Babylonian tradition of precise astronomical calculations.

Work on Tides

Seleucus made groundbreaking contributions to the understanding of tides. He correctly theorized that tides are caused by the Moon and noted variations in tidal timing and intensity across different geographical regions. Strabo credits Seleucus as the first to assert that the height of tides depends on the Moon's position relative to the Sun. This insight reflects the Chaldean tradition of meticulous observation combined with theoretical innovation, blending lunar cycle knowledge with heliocentric reasoning.

Legacy and Influence

Seleucus is remembered as one of the most influential Chaldean astronomers of antiquity. Strabo lists him alongside other prominent Babylonian scientists, such as Kidinnu and Naburianos, noting: "Seleukios of Seleukia was a Chaldaean too." (*Geographia*)

Although none of Seleucus' original writings have survived, his ideas are preserved through the works of later authors, including Plutarch, Strabo, and the Persian philosopher Muhammad ibn Zakariya al-Razi. Seleucus' contributions exemplify the Chaldean tradition of astronomical precision and its profound impact on Hellenistic science. His work bridged Babylonian and Greek intellectual traditions, highlighting the vital role of Chaldean knowledge in shaping the scientific foundations of the ancient world.

ENTRY 22

The Influence of Chaldean Sciences on Greek and Roman Scholars

The Chaldeans were renowned for their mastery of astronomy, mathematics, and advanced scientific knowledge. Their intellectual achievements shaped Mesopotamian civilization and deeply influenced Greek, Roman, and Jewish traditions. While the Chaldeans were repeatedly attacked and refuted in the writings of the Church Fathers, "Under the Roman Empire, many of the leading writers and thinkers in East and West were profoundly influenced by the Chaldean astrology and were convinced that it could ascertain the will of the gods and man's destiny."

Centuries later, European scholars such as John Flamsteed and William Kennett Loftus also recognized the enduring contributions of the Chaldeans, highlighting their pivotal role in the development of astronomy and science.

Greek and Roman Scholars Influenced by the Chaldeans

The Chaldeans' expertise in astronomy and mathematics was widely recognized, as noted by the Greek geographer Strabo of Amaseia in his *Geography* (16.1.6). He describes the Chaldeans as Babylonian philosophers and astronomers with distinct settlements dedicated to their scholarly pursuits:

> In Babylon a settlement is set apart for the local philosophers, the Chaldaeans, as they are called, who are concerned mostly with astronomy; but some of these, who are not approved of by the others, profess to be writers of horoscopes. (There is also a tribe of the Chaldaeans, and a territory inhabited by them, in the neighborhood of the Arabs and of the Persian Gulf, as it is called.) There are also several tribes of the Chaldaean astronomers. For example, some are called Orcheni [those from Uruk], others Borsippeni [those from Borsippa], and several others by different names, as though divided into different sects which hold to various dogmas about the same subjects. And the mathematicians make mention of some of these men; as, for example, Kidenas, Nabourianos, and Soudines.

Greek and Roman scholars frequently drew on Chaldean expertise in their scientific pursuits, solidifying the Chaldeans' reputation as "priests and astrologers." Notable figures influenced by their knowledge include:

- **Hipparchus**: Often regarded as the "father of astronomy," Hipparchus used Chaldean star charts to develop the first trigonometric table and calculate the precession of the equinoxes.

- **Diodorus Siculus**: His *Bibliotheca Historica* chronicled the achievements of the Chaldeans, emphasizing their role in astronomy.

- **Pliny the Elder**: In *Natural History*, Pliny credited the Chaldeans with pioneering observations of celestial phenomena.

- **Strabo**: His *Geography* highlighted the Chaldeans' contributions to astronomy and mathematics.

- **Eusebius**: The early Christian historian referenced Chaldean astronomical records in his writings on ancient chronology.

- **Flavius Josephus**: The Jewish historian echoed the Chaldeans' reputation for astronomy and their influence on early Jewish thought in *Antiquities of the Jews*.

Other thinkers, including Porphyry, Origen, Posidonius, and Pausanias, also acknowledged the far-reaching impact of Chaldean knowledge. Their contributions to science and philosophy shaped the intellectual traditions of the ancient world.

Tracing the Origins of the Chaldeans

Centuries later, European scholars recognized the profound influence of the Chaldeans. John Flamsteed, the first Astronomer Royal of England, acknowledged the Chaldeans as contributors to the early development of astronomy in his *Atlas Coelestis* (1753). In this work, Flamsteed references the "historical context of astronomical observations and cataloging," specifically noting "ancient cultures such as the Chaldeans, Egyptians, and Greeks." He highlights how the Chaldeans were "pivotal in recognizing and cataloging celestial patterns," laying the foundation for star cataloging and astronomical sciences.

In the 19th century, British geologist and archaeologist William Kennett Loftus encountered remnants of this ancient civilization during his travels in Mesopotamia (1849–1852). In his book *Travels and Researches in Chaldaea and Susiana* (1857), Loftus described meeting Chaldean tribes in the highlands of Kurdistan: "They are called Kaldani, or Chaldeans, who profess Christianity and are known as a brave and hardy race."

Loftus theorized that these tribes were descendants of the original inhabitants of ancient Chaldea, displaced into mountainous regions by the later spread of Semitic peoples. He also observed the Chaldeans' enduring intellectual reputation:

> The frequent mention of the Chaldeans as priests and astrologers may be attributed to their migration carrying with them advanced knowledge of the sciences. This early expertise in science and astronomy contributed to their historical reputation.

Loftus, overwhelmed by the grandeur of ancient ruins like Warka (Uruk), remarked:

I know of nothing more exciting or impressive than the first sight of one of these Chaldaean piles, looming in solitary grandeur from the surrounding plains and marshes... [Warka] incomparably surpasses all.

Chaldean Contributions to Science and Astronomy

The Chaldeans were pioneers in astronomy, mathematics, and science, earning a place in the intellectual traditions of ancient and modern civilizations. Their reputation as "priests and astrologers" was cemented in ancient Greek and Roman writings and later European scholarship.

Their legacy is not only preserved in the records of scholars they influenced, but also in the physical remnants of their once-thriving civilization. The enduring ruins of ancient Chaldean cities stand as silent witnesses to their ingenuity, while their intellectual contributions continue to inspire humanity's pursuit of knowledge across generations.

ENTRY 23

CHURCH OF THE EAST
(1ST CENTURY AD)

When the Church of the East was formed in the first century AD, its heartland lay in Mesopotamia (modern Iraq), Upper Mesopotamia, and northwestern Persia—regions once within the Parthian and later Sasanian Empires. According to tradition, it was founded by Saint Thomas the Apostle, together with his disciples Saint Mari and Saint Addai (Thaddeus of Edessa), as Thomas journeyed eastward toward India. Over the following centuries, the Church expanded far beyond its original territory, establishing flourishing communities across Persia, Central Asia, India, and even China.

In *A History of All Nations, from the Earliest Periods to the Present Time* (1852), the American historian Samuel Griswold Goodrich described the enduring memory of the Apostle Thomas:

> From tradition, and even written accounts, we learn that Thomas was the apostle of the East, acknowledged to be such by all the Eastern or Chaldean Christians. He was the first preacher of Christianity among the Hindoos, and founded the churches of Malabar, where, to this day, the ancient monuments, writings,

and traditions afford the most indubitable proof of his apostolic labors among them.

This passage reflects how both the Church of the East and the Chaldean Catholic Church trace their spiritual ancestry to the apostolic missions of Saint Thomas, linking Mesopotamia's early Christian communities to those of South India.

In modern times, the Church of the East continued this heritage under new circumstances. After the assassination of Patriarch Mar Shimun XXI Eshai in November 1975, his successor Mar Dinkha IV was consecrated in 1976. That same year, the church was officially renamed the "Holy Apostolic Catholic Assyrian Church of the East" (commonly shortened to "Assyrian Church of the East"). It then reintroduced a new official seal, replacing the earlier one inscribed, "Humble Shimun Patriarch of the Chaldeans."

Chaldean seal used until 1976

ENTRY 24

JULIAN THE CHALDEAN
(2ND CENTURY CE)

As the influence of Chaldean knowledge continued into the Common Era, it evolved and adapted to new intellectual and spiritual contexts. One of the key figures embodying this continuity was Julian the Chaldean, along with his son, Julian the Theurgist. Living in the 2nd century CE, possibly during the reign of Emperor Marcus Aurelius (161–180 CE), they significantly shaped Neoplatonic philosophy and the mystical traditions of late antiquity.

The Chaldean Oracles

Julian and his son are traditionally credited with authoring or compiling the Chaldean Oracles. These texts, written in Greek, are a collection of mystical and philosophical writings that blend Platonic philosophy with elements of ancient Near Eastern religious thought, particularly from the Chaldean (Babylonian) tradition. The Oracles focus on the nature of the cosmos, the relationship between the divine and human souls, and the process of spiritual ascent. They present a hierarchical universe where the material world is distant from the divine but accessible through theurgy—rituals meant to invoke the presence of the gods and elevate the soul.

Influence and Legacy

The Chaldean Oracles were highly esteemed in Late Antiquity and were considered almost as important as Plato's works by later Neoplatonists. They embody a blend of Hellenistic syncretism, combining elements from Babylonian, Persian, and Egyptian traditions. The word theurgy itself is coined in the Chaldean Oracles. Julian's teachings emphasize the transformative power of theurgy as a means to transcend the material world and align with the divine. The Oracles describe the transcendent First Paternal Intellect, from whom the Second Intellect, the Demiurge, comprehends the cosmos. A combination of ascetic conduct and correct ritual is recommended to free the soul from the confines of matter and to defend it against demonic powers.

Although the original texts have been lost, they survive in fragments consisting mainly of quotes and commentary by Neoplatonist writers. Later Neoplatonists, such as Iamblichus (c. 245–325 CE) and Proclus (412–485 CE), integrated the teachings of the Chaldean Oracles into their own interpretations of Plato's philosophy. As Franz Cumont famously said, the Oracles are the "Bible of the last Neoplatonists."

Theurgic Reputation

Julian the Theurgist is reputed by some pagan writers, including the 3rd- and 4th-century Neoplatonists, to have saved the Roman army from a severe drought during Marcus Aurelius' campaign against the Quadi. This reinterpretation replaced the Egyptian magician mentioned by the 2ndcentury historian Cassius Dio with Julian, likely to align the event with Neoplatonic ideals and the growing importance of theurgy.

ENTRY 25

CHALDEANS AND CHRISTIANITY IN CHINA, 400 AD

Christianity first reached China during the Han and Tian dynasties (the first three centuries CE). According to Chaldean writings referenced by Father Hwang, St. Thomas the Apostle is said to have brought the Gospel to both India and China during the early part of the first century CE. Father Hwang cites *Western History* to report that Archbishop Akeno of Chaldea established a vicar-general in 400 AD to oversee the Christian faith in China (*The China Review, Or, Notes and Queries on the Far East, Volume 20, p. 382*).

This early connection shows the critical role played by the Church of the East, historically linked with the Chaldeans, in spreading Christianity across Asia. The establishment of a vicar-general in China reveals the organizational efforts of Chaldean Christians to sustain their faith in regions far removed from their homeland, even under dynasties that largely adhered to non-Christian beliefs.

ENTRY 26

SAINT HIRMIZ CHALDEAN CHURCH (397 AD)

Built in 397 AD, Mar Hirmiz Keldani Kilisesi (Chaldean Cathedral) in Mardin, Turkey, stands as a symbol of the enduring cultural and spiritual legacy of the Chaldean community. Distinct from the Syriac Orthodox tradition, the cathedral houses one of the region's most significant collections of manuscripts, reflecting centuries of Chaldean Catholic scholarship. The collection, digitized in 2012 in partnership with the Centre Numérique des Manuscrits Orientaux (CNMO), includes 588 manuscripts in East Syriac, Arabic, and Garshuni. These works span hagiographies, linguistic texts, theological homilies, and secular literature, illustrating the intellectual and cultural vitality of the Chaldean tradition.

Written in a remarkable variety of languages—including Syriac, Arabic, Neo-Aramaic, and Persian Garshuni—the manuscripts reflect the cathedral's historic role as a center of learning and cultural exchange in the region. By preserving these treasures, Mar Hirmiz Keldani Kilisesi ensures that the legacy of the Chaldean faith and scholarship endures for future generations.

Saint Hirmiz Chaldean Church - 4th Century
Mardin - Turkey

ENTRY 27

Nestorius: The Controversial Archbishop of Constantinople (5th Century AD)

Nestorius was born around 386 AD in Germanicia (modern-day Kahramanmaraş, Turkey) in the Roman province of Syria. He served as Archbishop of Constantinople from 428 to 431 AD. His tenure coincided with a period of intense theological debates concerning the nature of Christ and the Virgin Mary.

Theological Controversy

Nestorius is most famously associated with rejecting the title *Theotokos* ("God-bearer") for the Virgin Mary, instead advocating for *Christotokos* ("Christ-bearer"). He argued that Mary gave birth to the human nature of Christ, not the divine essence itself, thereby emphasizing a distinction between Christ's divine and human natures. His position, however, was perceived by opponents as undermining the unity of Christ and led to widespread controversy, culminating in what is known as the Nestorian Schism.

Council of Ephesus and Exile

Nestorius's teachings were condemned at the Council of Ephesus in 431. Opposed by Cyril of Alexandria, the council branded his views as heretical and deposed him as Archbishop of Constantinople. Initially, Nestorius was allowed to return to his former monastery near Antioch, but political pressures led Emperor Theodosius II to exile him in 435 to the remote Great Oasis of Hibis (modern Kharga Oasis) in Upper Egypt. He spent the remainder of his life in harsh isolation, dying around 450 in Panopolis (modern Akhmim, Egypt). Despite his exile, his teachings endured through his writings and followers.

Legacy and the Church of the East

Following the Council of Ephesus, Christians who adhered to a Christology similar to Nestorius were expelled from the Roman Empire. These communities sought refuge in the Sasanian Empire (modern-day Iran and Iraq), where they flourished under more tolerant conditions.

Although these Christians are more accurately referred to as the Church of the East, they were derogatorily labeled "Nestorians" by theological opponents. While the Church of the East respected Nestorius as an influential figure in theological history, they did not adopt his teachings in their entirety. Instead, they developed a distinct Christology that emphasized the separation between Christ's divine and human natures, drawing from the broader Antiochian theological tradition that Nestorius represented, rather than from his specific doctrines.

ENTRY 28

THE CHALDEANS AND THE ADOPTION OF NESTORIANISM

Transition to Nestorian Theology

In 484 AD, the Church of the East officially adopted a Christological theology influenced by Theodore of Mopsuestia and Nestorius, marking a significant departure from other Christian traditions. While some Chaldeans aligned with this theological framework, others maintained their Catholic roots and ties to the Patriarchate of Antioch. Over time, the term "Chaldean" became intertwined with their cultural and historical identity, even as theological divisions deepened.

The Chaldean-Nestorian Debate

The terms "Chaldean" and "Nestorian" were often conflated, yet they carried distinct meanings. Chaldeans, as descendants of Abraham, rejected the term "Nestorian," which they saw as an external imposition. William Francis Ainsworth, a 19th-century scholar and traveler, documented their opposition to this label. He wrote:

> They protested against being called Nestorians, their true designation being Chaldeans. They said, "Nestor was the patriarch of the Greeks and not of us. Cyril and his followers were opposed to our Church because

we did not embrace their doctrines, and they calumniated us by designating us as followers of Nestorius. But our Church existed long before the schism of the Nestorians, and held by the same doctrine both before and after the patriarch whose name has been imposed upon us by a depreciatory ill-will."

Ainsworth further noted that the term "Nestorian" was applied by outsiders, particularly Western missionaries, who sought to elevate the significance of their conversions in the East. The Chaldeans also highlighted their theological independence and heritage. Ainsworth recorded their insistence on their connection to Abraham and their rejection of the Nestorian label:

> The name of Chaldeans expresses their relation to Abraham, who was from Ur of the Chaldees; and the name of Nestorian, he admits, is repudiated by the Chaldeans, yet he excuses himself for applying it to them on the curious grounds, that, throughout Protestant Christendom, the name of Nestorian is justly honoured, and there seems to be no good reason for [its rejection].

Observations by Riccoldo da Monte Croce

The Dominican friar Riccoldo da Monte Croce, who traveled extensively in the Middle East between 1288 and 1300, offered a nuanced view of the Chaldean-Nestorian Church. Immersed in their languages and traditions, Riccoldo observed: "These eastern Nestorians are all Chaldeans, and they pray and read in Chaldean."

He noted that many theological disputes between Latins and Nestorians arose from linguistic misunderstandings. Riccoldo wrote: "The Nestorians' disagreement with the Latins was purely owing to terminology that was lost in translation."

Despite these differences, Riccoldo admired their devotion and recognized their shared Christian identity with the Latin Church.

Joseph Wilmhurst wrote that Pope Paul V (1605-1621) wrote to Patriarch Eliyya, "A great part of the East was infected by this heresy [Nestorianism], especially the Chaldeans, who for this reason, have been called Nestorians."

Cultural and Liturgical Practices

The Chaldeans and Nestorians shared many cultural and liturgical traditions, though some differences emerged over time. George Percy Badger observed:

> The Chaldeans adopted certain practices from the Western Church, such as allowing lay baptism in emergencies, a practice not permitted among the Nestorians. The Chaldeans also translated liturgical texts into Arabic for their people, while the Nestorians relied on oral translations into their vernacular, Soorith.

Conclusion

The shared history of the Chaldeans and Nestorians demonstrates their enduring ability to preserve ancient traditions while adapting to new theological and cultural influences. Riccoldo da Monte Croce, Ainsworth, and others observed that the Chaldeans resisted externally imposed labels and remained steadfast in their identity, rooted in their connection to Abraham and the ancient Church of the East. The emergence of the Chaldean Catholic Church in the 16th century reflects their resilience and capacity to evolve while maintaining their distinct heritage.

Nestorian (Assyrian) Christian family, Mawana, Persia (early 20th century). *Library of Congress.* Catalog notes identify such families as **Nestorian Chaldeans** until the 20th century.

ENTRY 29

Discovery of the Chaldean Lost Scrolls

Discovery and Digitization

In a monumental achievement, over 800 ancient manuscripts from the Chaldean Catholic Patriarchate of Baghdad, in collaboration with the Hill Museum & Manuscript Library (HMML) and the Centre Numérique des Manuscrits Orientaux (CNMO), have been digitized and made accessible to the public. These manuscripts, primarily in Syriac and Arabic, are invaluable records of the Chaldean Church's cultural and theological heritage. Among them are some of the earliest known Syriac manuscripts, with origins dating back to 794 CE and 822 CE, offering profound insights into the early history of Christianity in the Middle East.

Significance of the Manuscripts

The rediscovery of these manuscripts reveals the Chaldean community's longstanding and active role in the development of Christianity. The texts provide evidence that the Chaldean community embraced Christianity as early as the 1st century AD, firmly rooting themselves within the broader Christian world even under the Roman Empire. The manuscripts also highlight how the Chaldeans were deeply integrated into the

Catholic tradition from the very beginning, further underscoring their influence as one of the earliest Christian communities.

The Chaldean Schism and Its Impact

The manuscripts shed light on the 5th-century theological disagreements between the Chaldean Church and the Roman Catholic Church, which led to a division lasting over a millennium. This separation, however, did not erase the Chaldeans' theological and cultural contributions. The texts suggest that had this division never occurred, the Chaldeans might have been one of the most powerful and influential Christian communities in the world today.

A Legacy of Resilience

The Chaldean Lost Scrolls are not just historical artifacts—they answer longstanding questions about the Chaldean community's origins, contributions, and resilience. These manuscripts provide a unique window into a chapter of history where the Chaldeans were early and active participants in the development of Christianity. They document a vibrant and influential community that maintained its identity and traditions despite centuries of challenges.

Global Access and Scholarly Importance

By digitizing these manuscripts, the Chaldean Catholic Patriarchate and its collaborators have ensured that this rich legacy is preserved for future generations. Scholars, historians, and enthusiasts worldwide now have unprecedented access to these documents, which deepen our understanding of early Christian theology, liturgy, and culture.

ENTRY 30

CHALDEAN CHRISTIANITY IN ABBASID BABYLONIA (9TH–10TH CENTURY CE)

In *The History of the Jews: From the Roman Empire to the Early Medieval Period*, Moshe Spiegel describes the social and religious life of Babylonia, the region later known as Iraq, during and after the rise of the Abbasid Caliphate. He notes that when the Arab conquerors arrived, "neither had the conquerors met resistance on the part of the Jews and the Chaldean Christians, who had been oppressed by the Sassanids for centuries," highlighting that these two ancient communities had long coexisted in what classical writers continued to call Babylon.

Spiegel situates this period—the 9th to 10th centuries CE—within a time of intense religious and intellectual vitality in Abbasid Babylonia, centered on Baghdad (ancient Babylon). He explains that theological debates and political currents within Islam affected other faiths as well:

> The rivalry of both freethinking Caliphs and Christians brought Babylon into the sphere of competition of confession. … The Chaldean Patriarch was competing in the Christian church of Babylon.

This passage shows that by the early medieval period, the Chaldean Christian community was already a clearly identifiable and organized ecclesiastical body within Mesopotamia, maintaining its own patriarchal hierarchy and playing an active role alongside Jewish academies and Muslim centers of learning. Spiegel portrays a cosmopolitan Babylon, or Iraq, where Chaldean Christians, Jews, and Muslims all contributed to the complex spiritual and intellectual culture of the Abbasid era.

ENTRY 31

Chonain, the Nestorian Christian (9th Century CE)

Chonain (Ḥunayn ibn Ishaq), a 9th-century Nestorian Christian scholar and physician, exemplifies the intellectual and cultural achievements of the Chaldean-Nestorian tradition. His life and work reflect the vibrant scholarly activity of the Church of the East during the Abbasid Caliphate, particularly in the fields of medicine, translation, and philosophy.

Biographical Highlights

- **Birthplace and** Early Life: Chonain was born in Hira, a city long associated with the Chaldeans, particularly during the early Christian centuries. His father, a perfumer, provided him with a stable upbringing, and Chonain displayed an early passion for learning.

- **Education:** He traveled to Baghdad to study medicine under John the Physician (Masuya). Despite initial setbacks, Chonain mastered Greek and subsequently began translating texts from Greek into Syriac and Arabic, becoming a key figure in the transmission of ancient knowledge.

- **Achievements:** Chonain authored more than 25 books on medicine and science, including influential translations of Galen and Hippocrates, and became one of the most respected figures in Baghdad's intellectual scene.

Why Chonain Was a Chaldean

By the 9th century, the terms "Chaldean" and "Nestorian" were often used interchangeably to describe members of the Church of the East, as established in previous chapters. Writers such as Bar-Hebraeus and others frequently referred to the "Chaldean-Nestorian" tradition as a unified identity, underscoring their shared theological and cultural heritage.

Chonain's birthplace, Hira, further strengthens the connection. Hira was historically a center of Chaldean Christianity and intellectual activity. Chonain's affiliation with the Nestorian Church aligns with descriptions of the Chaldeans as renowned scholars and translators within the Church of the East. As noted in one account, Chonain "was from the city of Hira among the Arabs, a follower of the Nestorian sect, who never ventured beyond the territories of the Greeks, Chaldeans, or Syrians." This demonstrates the geographical and cultural context in which Chonain operated, further situating him within the Chaldean-Nestorian tradition.

Legacy

Chonain's work bridged Greek, Syriac, and Arabic intellectual traditions, playing a critical role in the Islamic Golden Age. His translations preserved and disseminated the knowledge of ancient Greek philosophers and physicians, influencing generations of scholars, both Christian and Muslim.

Through his scholarly contributions and his role as a cultural intermediary, Chonain exemplifies the intellectual vitality of the Chaldean-Nestorian Christian tradition. His life and work are enduring testaments to the Church of the East's role as both a theological and intellectual cornerstone of the medieval world.

ENTRY 32

Ibn Wahshiyyah: A 10th-Century Muslim Scientist, Alchemist, Translator

Ibn Wahshiyyah (d. c. 930 CE), a 10th-century Muslim scientist, alchemist, and translator from Iraq, played a pivotal role in preserving and transmitting ancient Mesopotamian traditions. His full name was Ahmed bin Ali bin Al-Mukhtar Al-Nabati, though he is better known by the epithet *Ibn Wahshiyyah*, meaning "the son of the beast."

Identity and Connection to the Chaldeans

Ibn Wahshiyyah identified himself with the Kasdanians, a name etymologically tied to the Chaldeans. Jaakko Hämeen-Anttila explains in *The Last Pagans*:

> "The community with which Ibn Wahshiyya identified himself was the Kasdanians, whence his own gentilicium al-Kasdam. The name is obviously etymologically related to Chaldaeans, the variation -slid- / -ld- originally going back to Babylonian."

At the time, the term *Nabatean* (*Nabaṭī*) was used broadly by Arabs to describe rural populations, particularly Aramaic or Syriac speakers. Ibn Wahshiyyah's title *al-Nabaṭī* reflects his expertise in agriculture and his ties to these communities.

The *Nabatean Agriculture*: A Compendium of Ancient Knowledge

Ibn Wahshiyyah's most famous work, *The Nabatean Agriculture* (*Kitāb al-Filāḥa al-Nabaṭiyya*), is an Arabic translation of ancient Nabatean texts, some originally written in Aramaic. The compendium covers a wide range of agricultural and botanical knowledge, including cultivated plants, wild edible plants, and medicinal plants. The work's multilayered transmission—from ancient Mesopotamian sources through Syriac intermediaries into Arabic—underscores its importance in preserving pre-Islamic traditions.

Beyond Agriculture: Contributions to Science and Mysticism

Ibn Wahshiyyah's contributions extended beyond agriculture. He translated works on poisons and fragments of astrological and mystical treatises, including *The Book of the Secrets of the Sun and Moon*. One particularly intriguing work attributed to him is *The Treatise of the 93 Alphabets*, which explores magical alphabets and their interpretations. According to Yale University's *Echoes of Egypt*:

> The *Treatise of the 93 Alphabets* is ascribed to Ibn Wahshiyyah, and although the attribution is doubtful, we know that it circulated under his name as early as the tenth century. The topic of the booklet is a long list of magical alphabets, their interpretation, and their equivalence in Arabic letters. Most of these 'alphabets' are just fantastic inventions and look very similar to the 'magical letters' we find in other Arabic magical treatises.

Ibn Wahshiyyah's Dual Identity

Max Müller highlights Ibn Wahshiyyah's dual identity as both a Muslim and a preserver of pre-Islamic traditions: "The Chaldean, who lived about 900 years after Christ…He was a Muslim whose family had converted three generations only."

This duality is essential to understanding Ibn Wahshiyyah's significance: while he embraced Islam, he also acted as a custodian of ancient Mesopotamian heritage, ensuring that the wisdom of the Chaldeans and Nabateans continued to influence Islamic intellectual history. His works, especially *The Nabatean Agriculture*, highlight the enduring impact of Mesopotamian traditions on the scientific and cultural discourse of his time.

ENTRY 33

EARLY MEDIEVAL CHRISTIAN RULE (10TH–11TH CENTURY CE)

In *The Crusades, c. 1071–c. 1291*, historian Jean Richard describes the state of Eastern Christian communities in Mesopotamia during the centuries preceding the Crusades. He explains how these groups—Armenians, Jacobites, Nestorians, and Chaldeans—continued to develop church structures and liturgies under Muslim political authority.

Richard notes that Arabic increasingly became the lingua franca of the region and reports, "Arabic was already the normal language of the Chaldeans of Mesopotamia."

This observation situates the Chaldean Christian community as a distinct and recognized body within medieval Mesopotamia, maintaining their own ecclesiastical hierarchy and liturgical traditions during the early Islamic and Abbasid eras (circa 10th–11th centuries CE).

ENTRY 34

MICHAEL THE GREAT (1199)

In his monumental *Chronicle*, Michael the Great, the West Syriac Patriarch of Antioch (d. 1199), provides a detailed exploration of the ethnic terminology of ancient Mesopotamia. Drawing on sources such as Josephus and biblical genealogies, Michael identifies the descendants of Noah's sons as follows:

- **Chaldeans**: Descended from Arpachshad.

- **Assyrians**: Descended from Ashur.

- **Arameans (Syrians)**: Descended from Aram.

Michael explains that, while these groups have distinct lineages, they are collectively referred to by the ancient name Chaldeans: "All of them are generally called Chaldeans, by that ancient name," although more specifically, some are referred to as Assyrians (from Ashur) and Arameans (Syrians).

To Michael, "Chaldean" serves as an ancient umbrella term for the Semitic peoples of Mesopotamia, emphasizing their shared heritage and linguistic connections.

Western vs. Eastern Aramaic-Speaking Christians

Michael also reflects on the terminology used for Aramaic-speaking Christians in his own time, noting a distinction between the communities west and east of the Euphrates River. He writes:

- West of the Euphrates, Aramaic-speaking Christians (his Jacobite flock) are commonly called Syrians.

- East of the Euphrates, Christians of the Church of the East: "Are not usually called Syrians… but instead are of the races of Ashur and Arpachshad, that is, Assyrian and Chaldean."

Michael acknowledges this 12th-century distinction but also emphasizes the shared heritage of these groups. He argues that the ancient Assyrian and Chaldean kings—who spoke the same Aramaic language—should also be considered part of "our people" (Syrians) in a broader sense.

Chaldeans and the Language of Adam

Michael further connects the Chaldeans to the language of Adam and Abraham: "The Chaldeans today possess the original language of Adam which [the Hebrews] lost. Abraham was a Chaldean, and the mother tongue of Abraham, which Eber retained, today is held by we Chaldeans."

This statement is a testament that Michael views the Chaldeans as custodians of an ancient and sacred linguistic tradition, tied to the biblical patriarchs and the origins of humanity.

Chaldean Identity: An Ancient and Enduring Legacy

Michael's *Chronicle* is remarkable for its acknowledgment of the historical and regional distinctions between

"Western Syrians" and "Easterners" (Chaldeans/Assyrians). For Michael, "Chaldean" was both a historical term for the peoples of Mesopotamia and an enduring descriptor of the heritage of his eastern coreligionists. His vision of a shared Aramaic language and ancestry reflects his broader attempt to unify the diverse Aramaic-speaking Christian communities under a common identity.

ENTRY 35

SABRISHO IBN AL-MASIHI (1226-1257 AD)

Contacts with the Holy See were first initiated by the Chaldeans during the Crusades (1096-1291). The earliest attempt at uniting with Rome was made by Sabrisho ibn al-Masihi who served as the Patriarch of the Chaldean Church of the East from April 12, 1226, until his death on April 23, 1256.

Historical accounts, particularly the *Ecclesiastical Chronicle* of Bar Hebraeus, describe Sabrisho's ascension to the patriarchate as being influenced by political maneuvering. Specifically, he gained favor with the Abbasid caliph al-Zahir through bribery, a practice that reflects the close but often complex relationship between the Church and the political authorities of the era.

Efforts Toward Union with Rome

A pivotal moment during Sabrisho's patriarchate occurred in 1247, when he sent his vicar, Rabban Ara, to Rome to engage with Pope Innocent IV regarding the potential union of the Chaldean Church with the Catholic Church. Rabban Ara was consecrated as a patriarch in Rome, signifying a significant step toward reconciliation. However, the ultimate outcomes of these efforts remain unclear.

While these attempts did not achieve full unity, they indicate the Chaldean's long-standing aspirations to reconcile with the Roman Catholic Church. These efforts preceded the more widely recognized union attempt of 1553, which marked a formal division between the Chaldean Catholic Church and the Assyrian Church of the East.

ENTRY 36

CHALDEANS IN MEDIEVAL PISA (12TH–13TH CENTURIES CE)

During the height of Pisa's maritime power in the twelfth and thirteenth centuries, the city stood as one of the great commercial hubs of the Mediterranean, attracting merchants and travelers from across Europe, North Africa, and the Near East. Edward Hutton, writing in *Florence and Northern Tuscany with Genoa* (1907), evokes this cosmopolitan era, describing what Pisa looked like "in the days of her great power and prosperity" before the midthirteenthcentury decline that followed Frederick II's death in 1250.

He writes: "And to the horror of less fortunate cities, these streets were full of 'Pagans, Turks, Libyans, Parthians, and foul Chaldeans, with their incense, pearls, and jewels.'"

Though colored by the prejudices of medieval observers, this description suggests that Chaldeans—likely merchants or craftsmen from Mesopotamia—were among the many Eastern peoples present in the bustling ports of Italy. Their mention underscores Pisa's international reach and its role as a crossroads of Mediterranean commerce and culture during the medieval period.

ENTRY 37

YAHBALLAHA III (1281–1317 AD)

Yahballaha III, born Markos around 1245, became the Patriarch of the Church of the East in 1281. His tenure as patriarch unfolded during a period of significant political and religious challenges, including the persecution of Christians under the Mongol khans Ghazan and Öljaitü. Despite these hardships, Yahballaha III made notable efforts to strengthen ties with the Roman Catholic Church, recognizing the importance of Christian unity in the face of growing pressures from Islamic powers.

Profession of Faith to Pope Benedict XI

On May 18, 1304, Yahballaha III made a remarkable profession of faith in a letter addressed to Pope Benedict XI. In this historic correspondence, he acknowledged the pope's primacy over all of Christendom. This was a revolutionary theological concession for a leader of the Nestorian Church, which traditionally resisted recognizing the supremacy of the Roman pontiff.

However, Yahballaha's overtures toward unity faced significant opposition from conservative Nestorian bishops. This resistance ultimately prevented the establishment of a lasting union with Rome, despite his sincere efforts.

Diplomatic Engagements

Yahballaha III demonstrated his commitment to fostering relations with the West by dispatching envoys, including the Chinese monk Barsauma, to engage with European powers and the Roman Church. These efforts reflect the Chaldean Church's long-standing aspiration to reconcile with Rome, a desire evident in earlier initiatives, such as those by Sabrisho ibn al-Masihi in 1247.

Although Yahballaha III's diplomatic efforts did not achieve lasting unity, they set a precedent for future discussions. His work highlights the ongoing challenge of balancing theological, cultural, and political factors in the quest for reconciliation. Notably, after later union discussions in 1445, Andreas, Archbishop of Colossæ, remarked: "After obtaining from this prelate certain modifications of the Nestorian Liturgy, Andreas forbade the Latin Christians of Cyprus to treat the Chaldeans as heretics."

This exemplifies the persistent efforts of the Chaldeans to bridge theological divides and foster mutual understanding with the Latin Church.

ENTRY 38

THE LITTLE BOOK ON THE KNOWLEDGE OF THE WORLD AND THE CHALDEANS IN MESOPOTAMIA (1404)

In 1404, Giovanni (John), an Italian Dominican friar and Archbishop of the Sultanate of Sulthanyeh, composed his *Libellus de Notitia Orbis* ("Little Book on the Knowledge of the World"), a Latin account describing the geography, peoples, and beliefs of the Eastern world during his work as a Dominican emissary connected to Timur Lenk's court. Within his section on Mesopotamia, Giovanni identifies the Chaldeans as one of the prominent Christian populations in Baghdad, recorded alongside Arabs, Syrians, Nestorians, Armenians, and Catholics. He writes:

> Now, however, we must continue our work and speak of which peoples there are, how many they are, and what their names are according to modern usage— those who follow the sect of the Saracens. First are the Arabs, the most numerous, among whom this sect had its beginning, and under them are many provinces, including all of Africa, as will be noted in their proper places. Among the others are the Persians, Medes, Parthians, Chaldeans, Corassans, Gillans, Kurds, Turks, Turkomans, Tartars, Barri (or Iberians), Thati, and Zathacai. And although there are

many other smaller nations, they are included under these as under general categories, as will be discussed in their respective provinces.

Giovanni's brief but vivid passage reflects an early Latin attestation of the Chaldeans as a distinct Christian community flourishing in Baghdad. His testimony offers a rare window into the religious and social fabric of late medieval Mesopotamia, where Catholic missionaries, Eastern Christians, and local populations coexisted under shifting political powers on the eve of the fifteenth century.

ENTRY 39

1457 WORLD MAP

The *Fra Mauro Map* is among the most remarkable achievements of late medieval cartography. Created by the Venetian monk Fra Mauro around 1457, the richly detailed circular map combines classical sources with contemporary reports from travelers and merchants across Asia and the Middle East. Oriented with south at the top, it reflects the expanding worldview of Renaissance Europe.

In Mesopotamia, the map labels the region "Babylonia (Caldea)," preserving the association of Chaldea with the ancient lands around Babylon. This reference demonstrates that the idea of Chaldea remained part of learned European geography well into the fifteenth century, bridging classical, biblical, and contemporary understandings of the Near East.

ENTRY 40

The Legacy and Marginalization of the Chaldeans

Enduring Reputation and Misunderstanding

The Chaldeans, one of the most advanced and influential cultures of the ancient Middle East, were often misunderstood and marginalized due to their past association with "paganism." While the early Church distanced itself from their heritage, their intellectual achievements endured and deeply influenced Islamic and Jewish thought.

Historical Continuity in Southern Mesopotamia

As Jaakko HämeenAnttila explains in *The Last Pagans of Iraq*, the Chaldeans were synonymous with the Babylonians, and their traditions continued in southern Mesopotamia:

> The Chaldaeans are the same as the Babylonians the rest (baqiyya) of whom nowadays live in the lowlands (bata'ih) between Wasit and Basra in villages. They turn towards the Northern Pole and Capricorn (alJady) in their prayer.

However, their identity became tied to paganism, which led to rejection by Christian communities:

The term Chaldaean had too strong pagan connotations to be accepted by Christians for themselves. The term Chaldaean remained pagan in tenor.

Influence on Islamic and Jewish Scholarship

Despite this, Chaldean intellectual achievements were widely respected by Muslim and Jewish scholars. Some Muslim historians even claimed that the Achaemenid dynasty traced its origins to the Chaldeans. Their language, often linked to Syriac, was also believed by Islamic scholars like alSuyuti to be the language spoken by Adam after the Fall.

Jewish thinkers, including Maimonides, engaged deeply with Chaldean wisdom. HämeenAnttila writes:

> The case of Maimonides proves clearly that Jewish authors were aware of, and interested in, the Nabatean, or Chaldaean (Kasdanian), wisdom transmitted by Ibn Wahshiyya... Part III, especially chapters 29–30, of Maimodines' *Dalalat alHa'irin (Guide for the Perplexed)* shows how extensively Maimonides had read the *Nabatean Agriculture* and how seriously he took the book.

Transmission of Ancient Knowledge

The *Nabatean Agriculture*, translated by Ibn Wahshiyyah, preserved Chaldean knowledge of science and farming, acting as a bridge between ancient Mesopotamian traditions and later Islamic and Jewish scholarship.

Although the Church distanced itself from their legacy due to its past association with paganism, others celebrated the Chaldeans as masters of ancient knowledge. Their contributions to science, agriculture, and mysticism remain a testament to their lasting impact on intellectual history.

ENTRY 41

PERSECUTION AND THE LOSS OF CHALDEAN HERITAGE

The Chaldeans, along with Assyrians and Syriacs, have endured centuries of persecution and oppression, which severely impacted their ability to preserve their cultural and religious heritage. This persecution began with the fall of Nineveh (612 BCE) and Babylon (539 BCE) and continued under successive regimes in Mesopotamia, including the Median, Macedonian, Parthian, Sassanid, and later Muslim rulers.

The Mongol Invasions and the Destruction of Knowledge

One of the most devastating blows to Chaldean heritage came during the Mongol invasions of the 13th century. Hulagu Khan's conquest of Baghdad in 1258 resulted in the destruction of countless manuscripts and cultural treasures. According to accounts, the Tigris River ran black with ink as books and scrolls were thrown into the water. This loss represented not only the physical annihilation of Chaldean knowledge but also a severe disruption to their ability to transmit their heritage to future generations.

The Long History of Persecution

Christianity, which had been embraced by the Chaldeans in the 1st century, brought solace during periods of foreign rule but also became a source of hardship. Under the Sassanid Empire, Christians were viewed as potential Roman spies, leading to waves of persecution. The 40-year persecution under Shapur II (339–379 CE) was especially brutal, as Christians were targeted for their faith.

Following the Islamic conquest in the 7th century, Christians initially hoped for tolerance, as Muslims shared a belief in one God. However, policies like the imposition of the *jizya* tax and forced conversions gradually reduced their population. By the Abbasid period in 750 CE, the number of *jizya* payers had dwindled to a small fraction of what it had been under early Islamic rule.

The Ottoman Atrocities and Modern Persecution

The Chaldeans faced some of their most severe persecutions under the Ottoman Empire. The massacres of 1914, 1933, and later genocidal campaigns in the 20th and 21st centuries further decimated their numbers. Events such as the Simele massacre (1933) and the ISIS genocide of 2014 left lasting scars on the community.

The Resilience of the Chaldean People

Despite centuries of persecution, forced assimilation, and displacement, the Chaldean community has shown remarkable resilience. Their faith, language, and cultural traditions were preserved through the steadfast efforts of the Chaldean

Church. Acting as both a spiritual and cultural guardian, the Church safeguarded their identity, preserving manuscripts, liturgical practices, and education.

The ultimate saving of the Chaldean name came with the union with Rome, which legitimized their identity and ensured the survival of their heritage for generations to come.

ENTRY 42

The 1445 Cyprus Union with the Vatican

In 1445, Archbishop Andreas of Colossæ, acting on behalf of Pope Eugene IV, worked to reconcile the Nestorian Archbishop Timothy of Tarsus, who was residing in Cyprus, with the Roman Catholic Church. As part of this union, modifications were made to the Nestorian liturgy, and Archbishop Andreas issued a significant decree: "The Latin Christians of Cyprus [were] forbidden to treat the Chaldeans as heretics."

However, this union was short-lived due to theological, cultural, and political challenges, as the broader Church of the East resisted aligning fully with Rome. It wasn't until 1553, over a century later, that a more lasting union with Rome was established under Patriarch Yohannan Sulaqa.

ENTRY 43

PATRIARCHATE OF YOHANNAN SULAQA (1551)

In 1551, dissatisfaction arose among clergy and lay leaders over the hereditary succession of the patriarchal office, which had persisted for over a century under the leadership of Simeon bar Mama and his nephew, Simeon Denha. In response, a group of bishops from Arbil, Salmas, and Azerbaijan, along with prominent laymen, convened an anti-synod in Mosul. They elected Yohannan Sulaqa, a monk from the monastery of Rabban Hormizd, as their candidate for patriarchal leadership.

Encouraged, possibly by a Latin missionary, Sulaqa sought recognition from the Roman Catholic Church. Traveling to the Vatican, he was consecrated as Patriarch of the Chaldeans by Pope Julius III, marking the formal union of the Chaldean Church with Rome.

Upon his return, Patriarch Sulaqa consecrated two metropolitans and three bishops, strengthening the structure of the united Chaldean Church. However, his leadership met fierce opposition from Simeon Denha, the Nestorian Catholicos, who sought support from the Pasha of Diyarbakir. Sulaqa was arrested, imprisoned, and executed in 1555.

Despite his martyrdom, Sulaqa's efforts laid the foundation

for the Chaldean Catholic Church. His successor, Abdisho, Metropolitan of Jazirat ibn Umar, continued his mission. Abdisho traveled to Rome in 1562, where he submitted a profession of faith to Pope Pius IV and was invited to participate in the Council of Trent. Although he declined this invitation, his profession of faith was read during the council's twenty-second session. Abdisho returned to serve his people until his death in 1567.

While the lineage of Sulaqa's successors faced challenges, including the return of some Chaldeans to Nestorianism during periods of instability, Sulaqa remains a pivotal figure for initiating the formal union of the Chaldean Church with Rome.

Excerpt from Mar Yohannan Sulaqa's Letter to Pope Julius III (1551)

"Know this, our most exalted Father, that our priesthood has, from ancient times, originated in Rome, which is the seat of Peter, the Prince of the Apostles. However, since the order of Christians was disrupted by the sons of Hagar (i.e., the Arabs of Egypt), our path to you has been interrupted for a span of 300 years until this day."

Historical Note

Sulaqa's letter reflects his effort to emphasize the Chaldeans' ties to the Catholic Church. However, historical records indicate that early Chaldean patriarchs were subject to the Patriarch of Antioch, not directly to Rome. This claim of Roman origins likely stemmed from a misunderstanding of Antioch's role as part of the Roman Empire during early Christianity.

ENTRY 44

PIETRO DELLA VALLE AND SITTI MAANI (17TH CENTURY)

Pietro della Valle's Journeys and Encounter with the Chaldeans

Pietro della Valle (1586–1652), an Italian traveler, poet, musician, linguist, and member of Roman nobility, embarked on extensive journeys throughout the Middle East, Persia, and India, documenting his experiences with a keen eye for detail and a deep appreciation for diverse cultures. His travels brought him into contact with the Chaldean people of Mesopotamia, igniting a fascination that would shape his life and legacy.

Meeting Sitti Maani in Baghdad

In 1616, while in Baghdad, Della Valle met Sitti Maani Gioerida, a noblewoman of mixed heritage—her father was a Nestorian Catholic, and her mother was Armenian. This distinguished lineage provided Sitti Maani with connections to the broader Christian communities of Mesopotamia, including Chaldean relatives mentioned by other writers. Her remarkable beauty, intelligence, and virtue captivated Della Valle, sparking a passionate courtship that culminated in a marriage transcending cultural boundaries. As Della Valle's biographer notes, this alliance provided him with another reason to meet Shah ʿAbbās I, whose reputation for religious tolerance encouraged his vision of establishing a colony of Chaldean and Nestorian Christians at Isfahan under the Shah's benevolent protection.

Origins and Qualities of Sitti Maani

Born in Mardin, a prominent city in Mesopotamia, Sitti Maani was a member of the distinguished Gioerida family, widely admired for their devotion to the Christian faith. Her name, "Maani," derived from the Arabic term meaning "eloquence and intelligence," reflected her exceptional qualities. She was fluent in multiple languages, welleducated, and renowned for her wisdom, kindness, and piety.

Marriage and Shared Faith

Their union was rooted not only in love but also in a shared Christian faith. Della Valle admired the Chaldean heritage that Sitti Maani embodied, and she embraced the Latin Catholic tradition during their time together without abandoning her cultural identity.

Travels and Partnership

Sitti Maani accompanied Pietro on his extensive travels throughout Persia and other regions. Enduring the hardships of long journeys and wars with remarkable resilience, she became his equal partner in all things. In his famous travel letters, later compiled into *Viaggi di Pietro Della Valle il Pellegrino*, he described her as "The light of my life and a model of virtue, kindness, and strength. Her wisdom and beauty were unmatched, and her faith gave me courage in the darkest of times."

Faith and Charity

Sitti Maani also played an active role in supporting Christian communities, assisting the poor and guiding those who had strayed from the faith back to the Church. Her devotion and compassion left an indelible mark on those she encountered.

Death and Mourning

Tragically, in 1621, while in Mina, near the Persian Gulf, Sitti Maani passed away due to complications from childbirth. Overcome with grief, Della Valle had her body embalmed and brought with him on his travels, ultimately transporting her remains back to Rome—an arduous journey that took nearly four years. As Rocchi notes, Pietro della Valle had her body mummified and continued to travel with the corps until his return in Rome in 1626.

Funeral and Commemoration

Upon arriving in Rome, Pietro organized an elaborate funeral in her honor. She was buried in the Della Valle family chapel at Santa Maria in Ara Coeli, where a grand ceremony celebrated her life. Pietro also commissioned a publication, *Funerale della Signora Sitti Maani Gioerida della Valle (1627)*, which described her life, virtues, and funeral in great detail.

The publication praised her as:

> A noble woman of Mardin, whose beauty rivaled Rachel, whose prudence mirrored Deborah, and whose piety resembled that of Anna. She was a matron of exemplary virtue, a beacon of Christian faith, and a model of charity.

Legacy and Cultural Impact

Through his marriage to Sitti Maani and his deep engagement with the Christian communities of Mesopotamia, Della Valle not only experienced a profound personal transformation but also contributed to a greater understanding of Chaldean culture and history in Europe.

Sitti Maani Gioerida della

Pietro della Valle

ENTRY 45

NATION OF THE CHALDEANS (1617)

Printed in Rome in 1617, *De Chaldaeorum Natione* ("On the Nation of the Chaldeans") is one of the earliest works to describe the Chaldeans as a distinct Christian people. It reads:

> The Chaldean nation, descended from the ancient people of Mesopotamia, now lives chiefly under Turkish and Persian rule. Though their empire has long faded, they remain steadfast in the Christian faith, preserving the Syriac language and the ancient rites handed down from the Apostles.

ENTRY 46

THE SCRIBES AND WRITERS OF CHALDEAN HERITAGE

The Chaldeans have a long and illustrious tradition of writing and documentation, rooted in their Mesopotamian ancestry. For centuries, they meticulously recorded a wide range of phenomena, including astronomical and natural events such as the movements of stars and planets, eclipses, river levels, and weather patterns. This scribal tradition was integral to the socio-economic and cultural fabric of ancient Mesopotamian cities, particularly Borsippa, a prominent urban center.

As detailed in Ran Zadok's *The Scribes of Borsippa in the First Millennium BC: A Preliminary Survey*, the scribal community in Borsippa alone consisted of 1,727 identified scribes, each documented by name and family lineage. These individuals often held surnames, signifying their elite status within the local urban society. The scribes played crucial roles in administrative, religious, and scholarly activities, serving as the custodians of Mesopotamian heritage, particularly during the Neo-Babylonian period under rulers like Nebuchadnezzar II.

The Continuation of Chaldean Literary Tradition

Following the Chaldean Church's union with Rome in later centuries, this tradition of writing and preserving cultural heritage continued. Chaldean writers and scribes emerged as vital figures in safeguarding their identity and history. By documenting their experiences, theological insights, and cultural narratives, these individuals ensured that Chaldean heritage would endure through tumultuous periods of history.

Below are some of the most notable Chaldean scribes and writers who contributed to the preservation and propagation of their identity:

- **Joseph Adjutus (16th century)**
  - A notable writer and theologian, Joseph Adjutus is remembered for his works on Chaldean history and theology. His writings provided a vital link between Mesopotamian traditions and the Chaldeans' evolving relationship with the Roman Catholic Church.

- **Elias al-Musili (17th century)**
  - A groundbreaking figure, Elias al-Musili is recorded as the first Middle Easterner to travel to the Americas. His travelogue documented his journeys and observations, offering valuable insight into the experiences of a Chaldean traveler during the 17th century.

- **Maria Theresa Asmar (19th century)**
  - Known as "the Babylonian Princess," Maria Theresa Asmar was a writer whose memoirs vividly described her experiences as a Chaldean woman during the 19th century. Her works preserved vital aspects of Chaldean

culture, history, and the challenges her community faced.

- **Hormuzd Rassam (19th century)**
  - An archaeologist and historian, Hormuzd Rassam is celebrated for his contributions to the study of Mesopotamian history. His work unearthed key artifacts and texts that linked the ancient Mesopotamian civilization to the heritage of the Chaldeans.

- **Joseph Naayem (20th century)**
  - A Chaldean priest and historian, Joseph Naayem chronicled the plight of the Chaldean people during the early 20th century, particularly during the Christian Genocide. His writings shed light on the suffering and resilience of his community during this tragic period.

- **Mariam Raphael Romaya Nerma (1890 – 20th Century)**
  - An Iraqi journalist, educator, and pioneer, Mariam Raphael Romaya Nerma was born on April 3, 1890, in Baghdad. A Chaldean Christian from the city of Tel Kaif, she holds distinction as the first Iraqi female journalist, marking a turning point in the country's cultural and intellectual history. Through her work in education and the press, she opened new opportunities for women in public life and contributed to the early shaping of modern Iraqi journalism.

Legacy of Chaldean Scribes and Writers

These writers and scribes represent a continuation of the ancient Mesopotamian tradition of documentation and intellectual inquiry. Their works not only preserved Chaldean history and culture but also bridged the gaps between eras, ensuring that their heritage was communicated to both Eastern and Western audiences.

Chaldean Catholic bookbinders in Mosul, photograph, 1890.

ENTRY 47

JOSEPHUS ADJUTUS (17TH CENTURY CHALDEAN SCHOLAR)

Josephus was born in Mosul in 1602 into a Chaldean Christian family. His life took a tragic turn when both of his parents died in 1606, leaving him orphaned at an early age. He was subsequently sent to Jerusalem, where he was raised under the care of the Franciscan Friars Minor.

He began his formal education at a Franciscan monastery in Palestine, where he received rigorous training in theology, biblical studies, and languages. By 1613, he had completed his studies and emerged as a promising scholar. His academic journey continued in Europe, and in 1637, he earned a Doctor of Theology degree from the prestigious Collegium Bononiensis in Bologna, Italy. This marked the culmination of years of dedicated scholarship and theological training.

Academic Career in Europe

After completing his studies, Josephus traveled extensively across Europe, visiting cities such as Vienna, Prague, and Dresden, where he engaged with leading intellectuals of the time. Eventually, he settled in Wittenberg, Germany, where he was appointed as a professor at Wittenberg University, a prominent Lutheran institution.

Josephus's connection to Wittenberg is firmly supported by historical sources. As Burchard Brentjes notes in his 1977 article, *Josephus Adjutus, der Chaldäer zu Wittenberg*, Adjutus "took up residence in Wittenberg in the mid-17th century," distinguishing him as a Chaldean scholar who integrated into European intellectual life. Brentjes also contrasts Adjutus's permanent settlement in Wittenberg with other figures of the time, noting that he was unlike the transient "Arabian princes" who passed through the empire without establishing roots.

During his tenure at Wittenberg, Josephus underwent a profound personal transformation. He converted to Lutheranism, a decision that reflected his integration into the intellectual and theological currents of the Reformation. Referring to Wittenberg as his "new Jerusalem," he embraced his role as a scholar who bridged Eastern and Western traditions.

As a professor of Oriental studies, Josephus earned widespread recognition for his expertise in theology, biblical languages, and Eastern cultures. His fluency in multiple languages, including Syriac, Aramaic, and Arabic, made him a sought-after authority on Eastern Christianity and the ancient traditions of Mesopotamia.

Legacy and Contributions

Josephus Adjutus was a pioneer of Oriental studies, promoting Eastern languages, cultures, and religious traditions in Europe. He bridged East and West, attracting scholars from across Europe and spreading knowledge of Eastern Christianity. Wittenberg University honored him with a preserved wooden plaque, marking his lasting impact on scholarship.

Portrait of Josephus Adjutus, aged 40 (1647).

ENTRY 48

ELIAS AL-MUSILI, FIRST MIDDLE EASTERNER TO TRAVEL TO THE AMERICAS (17TH CENTURY)

Elias al-Musili, also known as "Elias of Babylon," was a Chaldean priest who embarked on an extraordinary journey in 1668, departing from Baghdad, then part of the Ottoman Empire. His remarkable travels spanned Europe and the Americas, making him the first documented Middle Easterner to reach the New World.

In the 17th century, Europeans also referred to Elias's people as "Nestorian" or "Chaldean," reflecting their perceptions of the ancient Christians from the region around the Tigris and Euphrates, near the historic city of Babylon. As noted in *The Secret Life of Elias of Babylon and the Uses of Global Microhistory*, Elias embraced these associations with the ancient world. When he was seen in Mexico City in 1682, a Spanish chronicler described him as "dressed like a Turk in a long black cassock and the white collar of a priest." Elias himself wrote about the impressive beard he maintained during his travels, which left a striking impression wherever he went.

Elias's journey began with his departure from Baghdad in 1668. Over the course of eighteen years, he lived the life of a wanderer, traveling through cities such as Rome, Naples, Paris, Lisbon, Madrid, Lima, and Mexico City. His travels brought him across empires—Ottoman, European, and Atlantic—and his name appeared in various records in an array of languages. In Spain, he was referred to as "Elias de San Juan," while others called him simply "Elias de Babilonia" (Elias of Babylon).

Travels in the Americas

In 1675, Elias departed from Cádiz, Spain, for the Americas, becoming the first Middle Easterner to explore the Spanish colonies in the New World. His travel narrative provides detailed accounts of his experiences in Europe and the Americas, offering a unique 17th-century perspective on global exploration. Elias noted the vastness and diversity of the New World, a region even St. Augustine had once believed to be uninhabited.

Rediscovery of His Manuscripts

Elias al-Musili's manuscripts, which chronicled his travels, were rediscovered in Aleppo around 1900. The Lebanese Jesuit Antoine Rabbath published the texts in the journal *Al-Machriq* between 1905 and 1906. These writings are considered the oldest Arabic-language account of the New World and remain a valuable historical document.

Modern Interpretations

Elias's life and travels continue to intrigue historians and scholars. His role as a cultural and religious ambassador highlights the interconnectedness of the 17th-century world. My book, *Elias al-Musili: A Chaldean Priest's Journey to the New World in the 1600s,* offers a comprehensive retelling of his story, reaffirming his identity as a Chaldean priest and illustrating his contributions to global exploration.

ENTRY 49

ALQOSH—A CHALDEAN TOWN AND THE TOMB OF THE PROPHET NAHUM

In his 1842 volume *Mesopotamia and Assyria, from the Earliest Ages to the Present Time,* Scottish traveler and author James Baillie Fraser describes the town of Al Kosh (now written Alqosh) as "entirely a Chaldean town," drawing on observations from the noted British explorer Claudius James Rich. Although Rich had not personally visited Al Kosh, choosing to proceed instead to the convent of Itabban Hormuzd, he recorded that its inhabitants were "a very stout and independent class of men, who can muster about 400 musketeers."

Fraser notes that the town was modest in size but historically significant as the birthplace and burial site of the Prophet Nahum, "the El Koshite," whose Jewish family had lived there during the captivity of Nineveh. For centuries, Al Kosh remained a spiritual center, attracting Jewish pilgrims from across the region to Nahum's tomb.

Born in Alqosh in 1849, Qasha Oraha Shikwana and his son Ishaq took this photo at a Mosul studio run by the Armenian Saffarian brothers in 1890. Oraha copied over 30 manuscripts and authored hymns, as well as treatises on astronomy, the psalms, and the Chaldean Catholic Church's liturgy. His ancestry traces back seven generations to Qasha Israel Shikwana, born in 1541. Oraha passed away in 1931 at the age of 82.

ENTRY 50

MARIA THERESA ASMAR: AUTHOR AND TRAVELER (19TH CENTURY)

Maria Theresa Asmar was a 19th-century Chaldean author, educator, and traveler, best remembered for her memoir *Memoirs of a Babylonian Princess*, published in 1844. Sponsored by Queen Victoria, to whom she dedicated her memoir, the work provides a rare firsthand account of the life and struggles of a Chaldean woman from Tel keppe during a period of significant political and social upheaval in the Middle East and Europe.

Education and Advocacy

In Baghdad, Asmar sought to empower women and improve their education by establishing a school for women. However, her efforts faced strong opposition from Western Christian missionaries, who bribed the Turkish government to revoke her license and take over the school. Frustrated and disillusioned by this treatment, she left the city and sought refuge among the Arab Bedouins.

During her time with the Bedouins, Asmar documented their daily lives in rich detail, covering everything from weddings and celebrations to their raids on rival tribes. Her accounts remain an invaluable source of information on Bedouin culture in the 19th century.

Hardships and Travels

Asmar's life was marked by tremendous loss and adversity. Her family fell victim to a plague and persecution for their Christian faith. She eventually found refuge with Emir Bechir, the governor of Lebanon, at the Beiteddine Palace. From there, her journey took her to Europe, particularly England and France, where she faced repeated financial struggles and fell into poverty after being robbed multiple times. Despite these challenges, she lived in Europe for twelve years, during which she wrote her memoir, supported by Queen Victoria.

Legacy

Maria Theresa Asmar is celebrated as a trailblazer in Middle Eastern literature. For modern readers, her life and work have been condensed and retold in my book, *Maria Theresa Asmar: A Chaldean Woman's Story During the 1800s*, which provides a comprehensive account of her journey, writings, and the broader historical context in which she lived.

Memoirs of a Babylonian Princess frontispiece (1844).

ENTRY 51

HORMUZD RASSAM: ARCHAEOLOGIST AND DIPLOMATIC PIONEER (1826-1910)

Hormuzd Rassam (1826–1910) was a Chaldean archaeologist, diplomat, and key figure in Mesopotamian archaeology. Born in Mosul, in what is now Iraq, Rassam came from a wealthy and influential Chaldean Christian family. Their prominence, coupled with their faith, made them attractive partners for British interests in the region during the 19th century. Rassam's older brother, Christian Rassam, was appointed Britain's first vice consul at Mosul in 1839, and their family's connections brought Hormuzd into the British imperial orbit.

Rassam's introduction to archaeology came when Austen Henry Layard, the renowned British archaeologist, visited Mosul in 1845. Layard quickly recognized Rassam's linguistic abilities, cultural knowledge, and administrative skills, making him an invaluable partner in the excavation of Assyrian ruins at Nimrud. Rassam's work as translator, paymaster, and overseer of a diverse and often-sectarian workforce was instrumental in the success of these excavations, which unearthed significant Mesopotamian artifacts.

In recognition of his contributions, Layard invited Rassam to England, where he studied at Magdalen College, Oxford, in 1847. Layard envisioned Oxford as a place where Rassam could gain "a good English education… and most important of all the inculcation of English principles and feelings." This opportunity solidified Rassam's role as a cultural and diplomatic intermediary, bridging Mesopotamian heritage and British imperial ambitions.

Chaldean Identity and Writings

Hormuzd Rassam took great pride in his Chaldean heritage and often emphasized the historical significance of his people in his writings and professional endeavors. In *Travels and Researches in Asia Minor, Mesopotamia, Chaldea, and Armenia* by William Francis Ainsworth, Rassam is described as uniquely qualified for the Royal Geographical Society's Euphrates expedition due to his "knowledge of the Turkish and Arabic languages," his missionary background, and his "claims of relationship among the Chaldeans." These attributes positioned him as an indispensable figure in the exploration and documentation of Mesopotamia.

In his own book, *Asshur and the Land of Nimrod*, Rassam devoted an entire chapter to the Chaldeans, highlighting their deep historical roots and cultural contributions to Mesopotamia. He argued that the title "Chaldean" predated the Catholic conversion of Eastern Christians, illustrating the enduring historical continuity of his people. This distinction was crucial to him, as it reinforced the Chaldeans' identity as an ancient and integral part of the region's history.

Rassam's pride in his heritage extended beyond his

academic work. In his correspondence, he frequently distinguished the Chaldeans from other groups, such as the Assyrians, while emphasizing their shared cultural and historical ties. For example, in a letter to the British Foreign Office, Rassam wrote:

"They are there now with their blood-relations the Chaldeans, and many of the native-born Arabs are also akin, and their attachment to the country is clearly exhibited when they hold annually their three days Fast of Nineveh (*Bautha Ninwaye*)."

This statement underscores two important points:

1. **Shared Heritage but Distinct Ethnicities**: Rassam acknowledged the interconnectedness of the Chaldeans, Assyrians, and Arabs through shared traditions and family ties, while affirming the unique identity of each group.

2. **Cultural and Historical Continuity**: By referencing the Fast of Nineveh, Rassam tied the Chaldeans to longstanding traditions, demonstrating their historical and cultural presence in Mesopotamia.

Legacy

Hormuzd Rassam's contributions to archaeology and his advocacy for the recognition of Chaldean heritage remain invaluable. His excavations unearthed some of the most significant artifacts of ancient Mesopotamia, while his writings celebrated the Chaldeans' historical and cultural importance. By emphasizing both their distinct identity and shared heritage with other groups, Rassam left a lasting impact as a preserver of history and a proud advocate of his people.

Mr. Hormuzd Rassam vide Layard's Nineveh,
a portrait study of Hormuzd Rassam (1854)

ENTRY 52

REV. JOSEPH NAAYEM: PRIEST, SCHOLAR, AND HUMANITARIAN (1868 – 1964)

Life and Witness

Rev. Joseph Naayem was born in Tel Kaif, near Mosul in northern Iraq, in 1868. He was a Chaldean priest who became known for his deep concern for his community and heritage. During World War I, Naayem served as a chaplain to prisoners at Fort Afion KaraHissar in Anatolia. His contact with Allied nationals led Ottoman authorities to suspect him of conspiracy, resulting in his imprisonment and torture. In his later writings, he described the widespread suffering of Assyrian, Chaldean, and Armenian Christians, drawing from what he called the experience of one who "personally suffered."

Advocacy and Publications

Following his release and escape, Naayem traveled through Europe and the United States, raising awareness of the persecution of Eastern Christians and seeking aid for what he termed the "martyred race." His most influential work, *Shall This Nation Die?* (1920) includes a preface by Viscount James

Bryce and offers one of the earliest eyewitness accounts of what are now recognized as the Armenian Genocides.

Later Years and Legacy

Naayem spent his later years in exile in Switzerland, where he continued humanitarian efforts and correspondence with church and relief organizations until his death in 1964. His testimony remains a foundational record in the study of the World War Iera destruction of Assyrian and Chaldean communities and a lasting testament to faith under persecution.

Rev. Joseph Naayem dressed as a Bedouin
as he escapes the Turks.

ENTRY 53

THE MODERN ASSYRIAN IDENTITY

The Role of Western Archaeology and Romanticism

In the mid-19th century, prominent Western archaeologists, including Austen Henry Layard, unearthed the ruins of ancient Assyrian cities like Nineveh and Nimrud. These discoveries captivated global audiences, reigniting interest in the Assyrian Empire. Layard, fascinated by the grandeur of ancient Assyria, speculated that local Aramaic-speaking Christian communities—the so-called "Nestorians"—were the last remnants of the Assyrian people.

Layard proclaimed these communities to be "as much the remains of Nineveh, and Assyria, as the ruins heaped as ruined palaces." Similarly, J.P. Fletcher described the Nestorians and Chaldeans as "the only surviving human memorial of Assyria and Babylonia." However, this romanticized connection rested more on Western perceptions and desires to link the ancient empire to contemporary populations than on verifiable historical evidence.

Missionary Agendas

Missionaries, particularly from the Anglican Church, further shaped the modern Assyrian identity. Seeking to distinguish

the "Nestorians" from Catholic Chaldeans, they began referring to them as "Assyrian Christians." W. A. Wigram, a
key Anglican missionary, popularized this term as part of a
broader strategy to emphasize an ancient lineage for these
communities. Yet, even Wigram admitted that the historical
link between modern Assyrians and the ancient empire was
speculative. W. E. Ainsworth, writing in 1840, observed that
the Nestorians identified themselves as Chaldeans and "descendants of the ancient Chaldeans of Assyria, Mesopotamia,
and Babylonia."

Scholarly Critiques of the Assyrian Identity

Absence of Continuity

One of the primary challenges to the modern Assyrian identity is the lack of historical continuity. After the fall of the
Assyrian Empire in 612 BCE, the name "Assyrian" largely
vanished from historical records. Greek historian Xenophon,
writing 200 years later, described the ruins of Nineveh and
Nimrud as deserted Median cities, with no trace of the
Assyrians. This gap in continuity suggests that the Assyrian
identity, though it may have remained, it was sparingly and
not well preserved by local populations over the centuries.

Self-Identification of Aramaic-Speaking Christians

Some claim that during the Christian era, Mesopotamian
Aramaic-speaking communities identified themselves as
"Suraye" (Syrians), i.e. Assyrians, but that's also disputed.
Most claim that Syrians is a derivative of "Arameans." These
communities belonged to the Church of the East, which re-
ferred to itself as the "Patriarchate of Seleucia-Ctesiphon."

The term "Assyrian" did not emerge in association with these communities until the late 19th century, further highlighting the externally driven nature of its revival. Readers can explore Yasmeen Hanoosh's *The Chaldeans*, to gain a deeper understanding of these issues and the complex interplay between external influences and local identity formation.

Complications with Chaldean Identity

In contrast, the Chaldean identity has a clearer historical lineage. It also has a number of prominent figures like Maria Theresa Asmar and Elias al-Musili, who identified as Chaldeans, never referred to themselves as Assyrians or claimed descent from the ancient Assyrians. Asmar, for instance, consistently used "Chaldeans" throughout her memoir, referencing Assyria only in a biblical or geographical context.

The Revival of the Assyrian Name

Adam H. Becker's *Revival and Awakening: American Evangelical Missionaries in Iran and the Origins of Assyrian Nationalism* (2015) provides a detailed exploration of the role American missionaries played in shaping modern Assyrian identity. Becker demonstrates how evangelical missionaries, arriving in Iran in the 1830s, worked with the "Nestorian" Church of the East—a marginalized, Aramaic-speaking Christian community in the borderlands of Qajar Iran and the Ottoman Empire.

Over six decades, these missionaries educated the community within the frameworks of Protestant piety and Western science, while also introducing them to scripture and archaeology. The community, in turn, used this instruction to link itself to the history of the ancient Assyrians, giving rise to a new national identity. This newfound identity was documented in nationalist newspapers like *Al-Fajr (The Star)* in 1906 and led to demands for autonomy, showing how external influences catalyzed the revival of an ancient identity in modern terms.

A more recent exploration of this debate is found in Joseph Hermiz's paper, *Origins of Assyrianism: American Missionary Encounter and the Origins of Assyrian Nationalism, 1906–1918*. Hermiz highlights similar themes, emphasizing how external missionary efforts forged an Assyrian identity, which was not rooted in uninterrupted historical continuity but rather in modern global contact and intellectual awakening.

Even Assyrian scholar Sargon Donabed acknowledges the problematic nature of these narratives, stating that these "popularly and often academically accepted" conventions about the Assyrian identity reduce it to "Nestorians from the Hakkari mountains in Turkey" or dismiss their self-histories as "nationalist polemics." This underscores the externally driven and fractured nature of the Assyrian revival.

Conclusion

This topic is complex and requires its own in-depth research to fully explore the root of the modern Assyrian name—none of which is the focus of this book. The focus here is that, if there is such significant academic debate surrounding the legitimacy of the modern Assyrian identity, how then can Chaldeans, with their distinct historical and religious evolution, be tied to that highly contested identity?

The point of this entry is that historical evidence does not support claims that Chaldeans are ethnically Assyrian. In fact, some scholars even argue that modern Assyrians are actually Chaldeans who were historically labeled "Nestorians" due to theological differences.

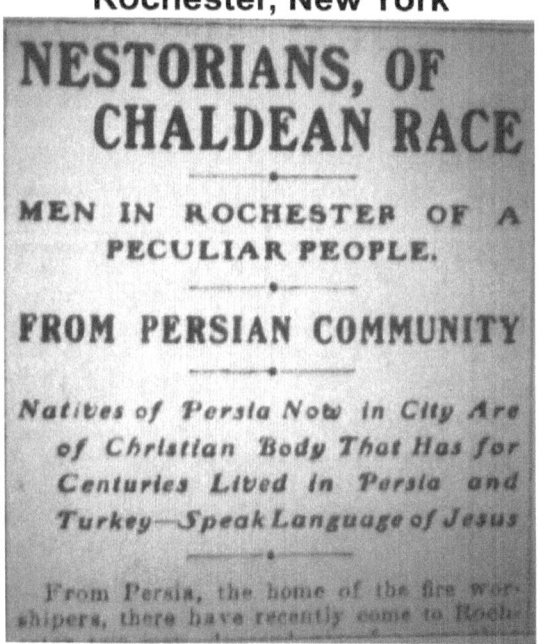

Nestorians, of Chaldean Race—Men in Rochester of a Peculiar People—From Persian Community.

Publication: *Democrat and Chronicle* (Rochester, NY)

Date: Sunday, August 20, 1905

Page: 20

Location: Rochester, Monroe County, New York, USA

ENTRY 54

EVIDENCE OF THE CHALDEAN PRESENCE IN MODERN AND HISTORICAL CONTEXTS

This chapter examines key evidence highlighting the historical and modern presence of Chaldeans in Iraq, emphasizing their enduring identity and contributions. Drawing from constitutional references, historical records, and recent demographic information, it explores how Chaldeans have maintained a clearly defined identity within Iraq's diverse cultural landscape. This evidence also illustrates the distinctions between the Chaldean and Assyrian identities, particularly in how the Chaldean presence has been consistently recognized through both historical documentation and modern institutions.

Article 125 of Iraq's Constitution

The Iraqi Constitution recognizes Chaldeans as a distinct nationality. Article 125 states: *"This Constitution shall guarantee the administrative, political, cultural, and educational rights of the various nationalities, such as Turkmen, Chaldeans, Assyrians, and all constituents, and this shall be regulated by law."*

This constitutional acknowledgment affirms the Chaldeans' unique identity and their inclusion among Iraq's national minorities. Notably, Chaldeans are listed separately from Assyrians, reflecting their distinctiveness as both a cultural and national group.

Historical Presence of Chaldeans: Mosul and Surrounding Areas in 1750 AD

Historical accounts from 1750 AD also provide vital proof of the Chaldean presence. According to The Annals of the Propaganda of Faith, Dominican Fathers reported the following:

- Chaldean Churches: 7

- Syriac Churches: 2

- Combined population of Chaldeans, Syriacs, and Armenians: 82,000

- Geographical coverage: Areas around Mosul and Siirt

These records illustrate the vibrant religious diversity of northern Mesopotamia during the 18th century, with Chaldeans prominently represented. The number of churches and adherents highlights their significant role in the region's Christian communities.

The 1957 Iraqi Census for Kirkuk and Sulaymaniyah

Another critical piece of evidence is the 1957 Iraqi Census, which recorded the population of Iraq's Kirkuk Brigade by sex and mother tongue. The census explicitly acknowledged Chaldean and Syriac as spoken languages, with a margin note clarifying: "This table reflects language, or national affiliation, from a royal-era census released in the republican period."

135

Notably, Assyrians are absent from this census, highlighting the clear recognition of Chaldeans and Syriacs as distinct groups and raising questions about the continuity of an Assyrian identity in the region.

The Presence of Churches in Baghdad

In July 2025, a Google search provided a snapshot of the distribution of Christian churches in Baghdad, reflecting the religious diversity of Iraq's capital. The count was as follows:

- Roman Rite Churches: 1
- Armenian Churches: 1
- Chaldean Churches: 9
- Syriac Churches: 4

The large number of Chaldean churches in Baghdad reflects the community's strong presence in the capital. This contemporary data aligns with historical records, showing the Chaldeans' continued influence and deep roots in Iraq.

Population and Church Statistics of Christian Groups in Iraq (Estimates)

- Chaldean Catholic Church—Represents up to 80 percent of all Iraqi Christians and maintains approximately 110 churches across the country.
- Syriac Churches (Catholic and Orthodox) —Account for about 10 percent of Iraqi Christians combined, with around 82 churches.
- Assyrian Church of the East—Comprises an estimated

5 percent (or slightly higher, depending on the source) and claims roughly 21 churches in Iraq.

Sources and Verification

The data presented above aligns with estimates reported by the following organizations and research bodies:

- U.S. Commission on International Religious Freedom (USCIRF) – A U.S. government advisory body that documents the demographics and conditions of religious minorities.

- Pew Research Center – A nonpartisan research institute that studies global religious populations, public opinion, and demographic trends.

- Aid to the Church in Need (ACN)_A Catholic aid organization that publishes reports on persecuted Christians and related statistics in the Middle East.

These organizations collectively support the approximate demographic proportions and church numbers shown above, with some variation depending on year and methodology.

ENTRY 55

THE CHALDEAN LANGUAGE:
A LEGACY OF ARAMAIC

For thousands of years, the term "Chaldean" has been closely associated with the Aramaic language, a Semitic tongue central to the cultural and religious identity of the Chaldean people. Spoken by Jesus in Galilee, this ancient language has persisted as a link connecting Chaldeans to their ancestral roots. Today, the Chaldean language—often called Neo-Aramaic or Sureth—continues to thrive among Chaldean communities worldwide, especially within the diaspora.

The Vatican's catalog of ancient manuscripts reflects the historical stature of the Chaldean language, grouping it alongside other classical languages such as Hebrew and Arabic. This archival recognition preserves an essential part of Chaldean linguistic heritage.

Historically, "Chaldean" and "Aramaic" were often used interchangeably. Writers, theologians, and explorers across centuries referenced Chaldean when describing Aramaic texts or speakers.

- John Owen (1616–1683), the English theologian, noted that Scripture was written in Chaldean characters so that "the truth could be more widely disseminated."

- Christopher Columbus (1492) reportedly brought a Chaldean translator on his first voyage to the Americas, reflecting the global reputation of Aramaic as a scholarly and sacred language.

- The Jewish mystic text *The Book of the Sacred Magic of Abra-Melin the Mage* (15th century) mentions being greeted in the Chaldean tongue during a vision.

- In the 19th century, newspapers like the *Cambridge Chronicle* advertised professors teaching Chaldean language courses.

- Mar Touma Odu (1897), metropolitan bishop of Urmia, authored a Chaldean dictionary capturing the richness of this evolving dialect.

- The Plantin Polyglot Bible (1568–1573) included Chaldean among its five languages, underscoring its place in global biblical scholarship.

- Charles Dickens (1859) in his book *A Tale of Two Cities* used the word Chaldean in his writing, specifically in the novel *A Tale of Two Cities* (Chapter 12), where he refers to the "Chaldean language".

The Chaldean Catholic Church also preserves this linguistic legacy through its use of Aramaic—or "Chaldean"—in liturgy. The Peshitta Bible, central to the Chaldean faith tradition, remains a living expression of that lineage.

Today, the Chaldean language is officially recognized by the International Organization for Standardization (ISO 6393: cld). While scholars may classify it as a dialect of Neo-Aramaic, Chaldeans proudly identify it as their own language—a symbol of faith, memory, and continuity. In diaspora communities, Chaldean churches and Roy Gessford, author of *Preserving the Chaldean Aramaic Language*, have made significant efforts to keep the language alive, including teaching Chaldean Aramaic to new generations.

Conclusion

The Chaldean language stands as a living testament to the endurance of a people and the continuity of an ancient legacy. From early biblical scholarship to modern cultural initiatives, it bridges centuries of history and strengthens the cultural identity of Chaldeans around the world.

ENTRY 56

DNA TESTING

DNA testing, though a relatively young scientific field, has seen remarkable advancements since its inception in the 1980s. While its origins in genetics date back to the 1950s, its practical applications have rapidly evolved over the past 20 years. Despite its usefulness in uncovering genetic markers and tracing population history, DNA testing cannot definitively determine an individual's ethnic or historical identity, such as "Assyrian" or "Chaldean." This limitation arises from the complex interplay between genetics, history, and identity.

Key Reasons Why DNA Testing Cannot Define Ethnic Identity

1. DNA and Ethnic Labels

DNA testing provides insights into shared genetic markers across populations, but it cannot assign individuals to historical ethnic categories like "Assyrian" or "Chaldean." Ethnic identities are social constructs influenced by language, culture, religion, and history, rather than purely genetics.

- **Shared Genetic Similarities:**

    Modern Assyrians and Chaldeans exhibit genetic similarities due to their geographic origins in

Mesopotamia. However, this does not confirm direct descent from ancient Assyrians or Chaldeans.

- **Broad Ancestral Results:**

  DNA testing may reveal Middle Eastern ancestry but cannot differentiate between ancient empires or modern ethnic groups.

2. Historical Narratives and Genetic Interpretation

DNA results are sometimes influenced by historical assumptions and self-reported ethnic identities. If historical research is biased or inaccurate, it can lead to flawed genetic interpretations.

- **Reliance on Historical Assumptions:**

  Many DNA studies depend on self-reported ethnic labels or historical narratives. If these narratives are flawed, the conclusions drawn from the genetic data will also be unreliable.

- **Modern Labels in Ancient Contexts:**

  Terms like "Assyrian" or "Chaldean" used in DNA studies often reflect modern identities rather than ancient ones, especially when there is no unbiased historical context.

3. Genetics Cannot Prove Cultural Continuity

Genetic links to ancient populations do not equate to cultural or historical continuity.

- **Assimilation of Ancient Populations:**

After the collapse of the Assyrian Empire in 612 BCE, its population was assimilated into various groups over centuries. No single modern group can exclusively claim to be "Assyrian descendants" based on DNA alone.

- **Cultural Identity Over Lineage:**

  Modern identities such as "Assyrian" or "Chaldean" are shaped by religious, linguistic, and historical factors rather than direct genetic inheritance.

4. Risks of Manipulated Historical Narratives

Tampering with historical research can distort how DNA results are interpreted, leading to the reinforcement of biased narratives.

- **Impact of Biased Sources:**

  If unreliable sources claim that all Mesopotamian Christians are "Assyrians," DNA studies might adopt this narrative, ignoring the distinct identities of groups such as Chaldeans.

- **Lack of Peer-Reviewed Studies:**

  Without unbiased, peer-reviewed studies grounded in historical accuracy, DNA interpretations may perpetuate false claims rather than clarify identity.

Conclusion

DNA testing is an invaluable tool for tracing ancestry and understanding population history, but it cannot definitively determine whether someone is "Assyrian" or "Chaldean" in a historical or ethnic sense. These identities are rooted in cultural, linguistic, and religious heritage rather than genetics alone. Furthermore, when historical research has been manipulated or biased, reliance on DNA testing without proper historical context can lead to misinterpretation. Ultimately, while DNA can shed light on where someone's ancestors may have lived, it cannot define who they are.

ENTRY 57

THE THRONES AND PALACES OF BABYLON AND NINEVEH (1876)

In his travel narrative *The Thrones and Palaces of Babylon and Nineveh* (1876), Bishop John Philip Newman recounts his journey through Mesopotamia and his encounters with the Chaldean Christians of Baghdad and Mosul. He recognized them as a distinct, ancient people within their ancestral homeland: "The Chaldean community to which I belonged is rightly esteemed the most ancient portion of the population... Our ancestors were the Chaldeans, or Assyrians, mentioned in the Bible."

Newman emphasized their continuity of name and language:

> The language which is used by the Chaldeans is known in Europe by the name of Syriac; but we ourselves call it Chaldean.

> Both Armenians and Kurds inhabit the same country now, and why not the Chaldeans? ... Why should the Armenians be called Armenians, but the Chaldeans merely Nestorians?

Newman's account confirms that, even in the nineteenth century, Western observers acknowledged the Chaldeans as a continuous nation—defined by geography, language, and faith in the heart of Mesopotamia.

Modern Interpretation. Bishop Mar Sarhad Y. Jammo's *Chaldean Identity in Historical Documents* (20th c.) consolidates these testimonies through papal decrees, archival letters, and ancient liturgical texts. He shows that "Chaldean" was selfused centuries before the 16thcentury Roman Union—appearing in martyrs' songs, patriarchal seals, and Vatican records. His research affirms that authors like Newman echoed an unbroken line of Chaldean identity rooted in Mesopotamian civilization.

Chaldean Catholics in Mardin, 1904

The photograph of Chaldean Catholics in Mardin from 1904 was originally published in an album by the French Capuchin mission. It was edited by a friar named Raphaël.

More specifically:

- The photo was featured in the Album of the French mission, 1904.

- It was later reprinted in the book Arménie: Il y'a mille ans, Ani.

- The image can be found in collections and archives such as the Virtual Genocide Memorial, which details the sources for images of Christian minorities in the Ottoman Empire.

ENTRY 58

CHALDEANS IN ARGENTINA

Discovery of a Forgotten Community

In October 2022, Dr. Paulo Botta from the Pontifical Catholic University of Argentina, reached out to me as the executive director of the Chaldean Cultural Center about a forgotten Chaldean community in northern Argentina. These families, who emigrated between 1900 and 1930 from villages near Lake Urmia in Iran, identified as "Kaldani" and spoke Syriac at home until the 1980s. Their journey was marked by hardship, with many fleeing persecution during World War I and the Russian Revolution.

Faith and Cultural Preservation

Despite assimilation into Argentina's multicultural society, these Chaldeans retained their Catholic faith and cultural pride, as seen in Syriac inscriptions on gravestones in El Carmen. Families like Abraham, Kamandaro, and Guibarguis represent a piece of the global Chaldean diaspora. This research proves that Chaldeans around the world proudly preserve their ethnic and cultural identity.

Research Collaboration

We collaborated on a project that shed light on this

community. I ended up writing an article about them for *The Chaldean News*, and the CCC sponsored Dr. Botta's trip to their town to interview them about their ancestral journey to Argentina. You can learn more by reading *"The Lost Tribe"* in *The Chaldean News*.

ENTRY 59

CHALDEANS IN INDIA

Ancient Trade Connections between Mesopotamia and India

Trade between the Indus Valley Civilization and Mesopotamia dates back to at least the third millennium BCE, during the Sumerian and Akkadian periods. This was primarily a maritime network extending through the Persian Gulf and the Arabian Sea.

During the Chaldean period (Neo-Babylonian Empire, c. 626–539 BCE), the Chaldeans controlled much of the Persian Gulf trade. Luxury goods such as pearls, spices, and timber from India were imported into Babylon. These exchanges were facilitated by a network of merchants from various coastal communities around the Gulf. While Babylonian records confirm trade with eastern regions, they do not suggest that ethnic Chaldeans themselves traveled extensively to India.

Roots of Chaldean Christianity in India

Centuries later, the Chaldean Christian presence in India emerged, closely tied to ancient trade routes and early missionary activity. A key witness to this enduring connection is the *Marth Mariam Cathedral* in Thrissur, Kerala — a Chaldean Syrian Church established in 1814. Kerala, thriving as a global trade center, was already flourishing when St. Thomas arrived in 52 A.D. to spread the Gospel.

Ancestry and Testimony of Modern Chaldean Catholics

Chaldean Catholics in Kerala, such as Mr. Roji Matthew, trace their ancestry to settlers from the Middle East. Matthew affirms this heritage, stating, "Our bishops came from Babylonia, and our priests were the same as the Chaldean priests." His testimony highlights the longstanding ties between the Chaldean Church in Mesopotamia and the Christian community of India.

Even early records describe the Christians of Malabar as "Chaldeans" or "Nestorians." The *Corrected Missal of the Chaldeans or Nestorians of Malabar*, preserved in the Vatican's Assemanian Library (*Codices Syriaci*), documents their liturgical rites in Syriac, reflecting the deep roots of Chaldean tradition in India.

Historical Challenges

The Chaldean identity in India faced pressures during the Portuguese Latinization policies beginning in 1498, which sought to replace Syriac practices with Latin ones. Despite these challenges, many families, like that of Mr. Matthew, preserved their Syriac heritage while adopting certain Latin practices for survival.

Leaders such as Bishop Mar Aprem Mooken, consecrated

in Baghdad in 1968, have played a crucial role in sustaining the Syriac traditions of the Chaldean Church in India. Contemporary initiatives, including the *Aramaic Project*, continue to promote the preservation of the Syriac language and liturgy, strengthening the connection between the Chaldeans of India and their global diaspora.

Enduring Legacy

The Chaldean presence in India stands as a powerful testament to the global reach of Chaldean identity and heritage. From the ancient trade routes of Mesopotamia to the modern Chaldean Syrian Church, this enduring tradition exemplifies a people united through faith, language, and culture.

To learn more, see my article "Chaldean Catholics in India" published in The Chaldean News.

ENTRY 60

REDISCOVERY OF CHALDEAN HERITAGE

Dr. Ali Eli, a university professor from Nasiriyah —the ancient city of Ur — represents a growing movement of Iraqis rediscovering their Chaldean heritage. After questioning his roots for over 25 years, Dr. Eli's research into historical texts, genealogical records, and traditions led him to confirm his Chaldean descent and embrace the identity of his ancestors.

Cultural Initiatives and Community Building

This personal discovery inspired Dr. Eli to establish cultural initiatives like *Shabab AlKaldan* (*Chaldean Youth*) and *Nisa' AlKaldan* (*Chaldean Women*) to preserve and promote Chaldean traditions in Iraq. His mission includes fostering unity, empowering women, and celebrating the Chaldean heritage through art, education, and interfaith dialogue.

Expanding the Mission

Despite challenges in a conflictladen region, Dr. Eli's efforts have uncovered over a thousand Iraqis' Chaldean roots and connected them with their identity. His collaboration with his son, Dr. Mohammed Ali, has expanded these efforts globally, ensuring the resilience and survival of Chaldean culture.

Enduring Legacy

This remarkable journey highlights the enduring legacy of the Chaldean people and their ability to inspire pride and unity across generations. To learn more, read my article "From Discovery to Legacy" in *The Chaldean News*.

ENTRY 61

A Chaldean in Afghanistan

At the suggestion of Professor Yasmeen Hanoosh, Sheila Turabaz, a woman who lives in the Netherlands, reached out to me, explaining that she was trying to locate Chaldean families to whom she might be genetically connected. Through DNA testing, Sheila had made an astonishing discovery—she is of Chaldean descent. I introduced her to the editors of *The Chaldean News*, who published her remarkable story, *"From the Nineveh Plains to Kabul."*

The article recounts the rediscovery of a forgotten Chaldean lineage that became part of 19thcentury Afghanistan's ruling dynasty. Sheila, a secondgeneration Afghan woman born and raised in the West, uncovered this connection not through family archives but through DNA matches with more than 265 Chaldeans across the global diaspora—particularly in the United States, Canada, Australia, and Europe.

The DNA Link

Using commercial genetic testing, Sheila identified undeniable links between her Pashtun Mohammadzai ancestry—an elite Afghan royal house—and Chaldeans from northern Iraq. Many of her matches trace their roots to Tel Keppe, Alqosh, and Mosul, with recurring surnames such as Abbo, Hanna, Putrus, and Younan. Further populationgenetic analysis confirmed that this Chaldean ancestry likely originated from a woman who entered her family line during the mid19th century.

A Forgotten Chaldean Ancestor

The missing link appears to be the wife of Sardar Mohammad Husain Khan, Sheila's greatgreatgrandfather, whose lineage is otherwise thoroughly documented. Her identity was absent from both official and family records, a silence that suggests she may have been an outsider—possibly the Chaldean woman whose DNA is still present in the family today. Elite Afghan households often forged alliances through intermarriage, including marriages with nonPashtun and Christian women, making this scenario historically plausible.

Christianity in 19thCentury Afghanistan

During the 19th century, Christians—often generically labeled as "Armenians"—lived in small but visible communities in cities like Kabul and Kandahar. It is very likely that the Chaldean woman's true identity was obscured under this generalized label, reflecting how Christian minorities were often grouped together in local and Ottoman records.

A Shared Legacy

Sheila Turabaz's discovery offers a profound reminder of how the Chaldean story extends far beyond Mesopotamia.

Her ancestor's journey from the Nineveh Plains to Afghanistan illustrates the remarkable resilience and adaptability that have long defined Chaldean history—a history carried not only through faith and culture, but now revealed through science.

EPILOGUE

My journey to uncover and document the Chaldean story has taken me across continents and disciplines. I have spoken with scholars, linguists, archaeologists, historians, and theologians—each shedding light on different facets of Mesopotamia's deep and multifaceted past. Among them were Geoffrey Khan, Amanda Podany, Howard Lupovitch, PaulAlain Beaulieu, James Toma, Yasmeen Hanoosh, Robert Dekelaita, Elizabeth Knott, Ali Bnayan, and Jaafar Jotheri, along with many others whose expertise enriched this research beyond measure. Not one of them asserted that the Chaldeans are ethnically Assyrian and no credible historical or scholarly evidence supports this notion.

Some modern movements have attempted to merge or obscure these identities, and they claim, repeatedly, "Chaldeans are Assyrians." But repetition cannot make an unproven statement true. The historical record provides no definitive link connecting the Chaldeans to direct descent from the ancient Assyrians; rather, it affirms that the Chaldeans represent a distinct strand within Mesopotamia's long continuum of civilizations.

Through this long and meticulous exploration, one truth has emerged with clarity: the Chaldean name has endured. Despite centuries of upheaval, shifting political systems, and evolving narratives of identity, the Chaldeans have preserved their faith, their language, and their culture. Their name remains a living testament to a people whose roots reach back to ancient Mesopotamia—a people who continue to thrive in the modern world while honoring the legacy of their ancestors. The writings of Ray Kamoo summarize this continuity powerfully:

> The name "Chaldeans," as applied in the last five centuries to Aramaicspeaking people of Mesopotamia, is meant to indicate their linkage to ancient Mesopotamian ancestry and culture. In history, Chaldean was the last universally acknowledged term to express Mesopotamian identity. Chaldeans, since 1000 B.C.E., were Aramaic tribes; their language, and the Babylonian culture that peaked with them, are the most precious legacy that is kept alive today with contemporary Chaldeans.

Today, the Chaldeans remain a distinct and officially and globally recognized people with a long, welldocumented history in Iraq. Within the broader family of Middle Eastern Christians—Chaldean, Assyrian, Aramean, and Syriac—each has its own story and heritage. Honoring these distinctions and allowing every community to define itself truthfully and without erasure is the truest way to preserve their shared legacy.

As this chapter closes, may it serve as a reminder that history lives not only in texts and ruins but also in the hearts of those who keep their heritage alive. The Chaldean people—heirs of a name, a faith, and a culture that has outlasted empires—stand today as proof that truth, when grounded in evidence and carried with dignity, never disappears.

To explore more images, illustrations, background facts, and videos connected to this work, visit ChaldeanChronicles.com.

"A Chaldean Lady" Creation Date: 1782 Creator: Charles West, John Boydell Type of Item: Crayon Providing Institution: National Gallery of Denmark (Statens Museum for Kunst)

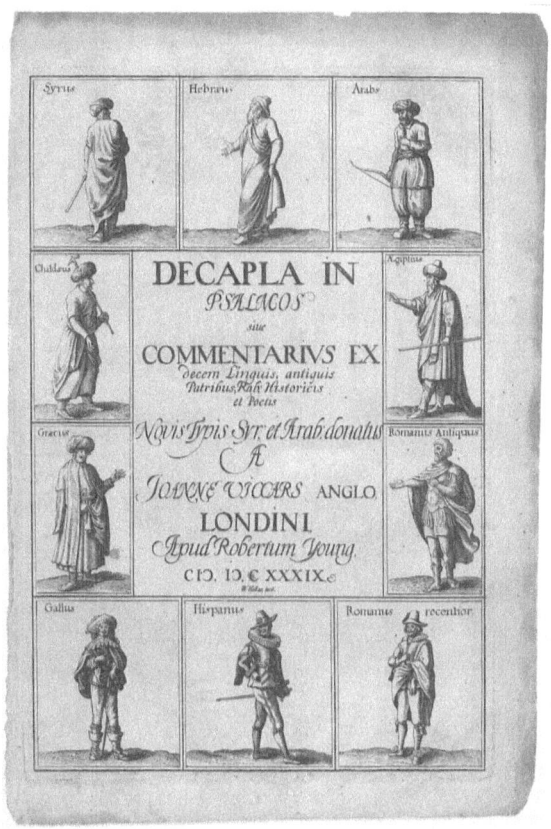

"Chaldean Man" from Title Page: Decapla in Psalmos (1639) Title page featuring text surrounded by ten portraits representing men of different nationalities: a Syrian, a Hebrew, an Arab, a Chaldean, an Egyptian, a Greek, an Ancient Roman, a Gaul, a Spaniard, and a Modern Roman.

Etching by Wenceslaus Hollar (Bohemian, 1607–1677) The Metropolitan Museum of Art, New York

NOTES

Introduction

- Gitbreth. "Father Augustine, Nineveh–Chaldean Monk." *X* (formerly *Twitter*). Accessed at x.com/gitbreth/status/1940873723957203338.

- "Chaldean Catholics." *Wikipedia.*

- "Category: Controversies in India." *Wikipedia.*

- "Could India Block Wikipedia? Unpacking the Latest Controversy." *TechGi – TechGig.*

- "Ideological Bias on Wikipedia."

- "Criticism of Wikipedia."

1: Who Are the Chaldeans?

- Byrne, Rhonda. *The Secret.* New York: Atria Books, 2006, pp. 5–6.

- Blavatsky, Helena Petrovna. *Isis Unveiled: A MasterKey to the Mysteries of Ancient and Modern Science and Theology,* Vol. I – *Science,* 4th ed. New York: J. W. Bouton, 1878, p. 50.

2: Abraham's Lineage and the Chaldeans

- *YouTube.* "The Origins of Abraham and the Chaldeans." Accessed at www.youtube.com/watch?v=_zYPmUPoWu0&t=121s.

- *Genesis* 11:31.

- *Genesis* 10:22–24.

- *Book of Jubilees* 11:13.

- *Gospel of Luke.*

- Flavius Josephus. *Antiquities of the Jews.*

3: Biblical and Early Christian Perspectives on the Chaldeans

- Lee, Adrian. *How to Be a Christian Psychic: What the Bible Says about Mediums, Healers and Paranormal Investigators.* 2nd ed. Wisdom Editions, 2022.

- Phillips, George. *The Doctrine of Addai, the Apostle.* London: Trübner & Co., 1876, p. 34.

- Wellhausen, Julius. *Prolegomena zur Geschichte Israels.* Berlin: G. Reimer, 1883, pp. 35-36.

4: First Mention in Archaeology (9th Century BCE)

- Grayson, A. Kirk. *Assyrian Rulers of the Early First Millennium BC II (858–745 BC).* Toronto, 1996. Accessed at http://oracc.org/riao/Q004619/.

- Luukko, Mikko. *Correspondence of TiglathPileser III and Sargon II.* Accessed at http://oracc.org/saao/ P224432/.

- Reynolds, Frances. *The Babylonian Correspondence of Esarhaddon.* Accessed at http://oracc.org/saao/ P237839/.

5: The Assyrian Deportation of the Chaldeans (10th–9th Century BCE)

- "Neo-Assyrian Empire Resettlement Policy." *Wikipedia.*

- Radner, Karen. "Mass Deportation: The Assyrian Resettlement Policy." *Assyrian Empire Builders.* University College London, 2012. Retrieved from oracc.museum.upenn.edu/saao/aebp/essentials/governors/massdeportation/.

- Podany, Amanda H. *Weavers, Scribes, and Kings: A New History of the Ancient Near East.* Oxford University Press, 2022, p. 443.

6: The Chaldean Tribes and the Nimrud Letters (9th–7th Century BCE)

- Grayson, A. Kirk, Grant Frame, and Jamie Novotny. *RINAP Project.* Accessed at http://oracc.org/rinap/Q003475/.

- Hannona, Habib. *The Chaldean Exodus.* 2022.

- Saggs, H. W. F. "Chaldeans in the Nimrud Letters." *Wiener Zeitschrift für die Kunde des Morgenlandes* 86 (1996): 379–390 University of Vienna, Department of Oriental Studies. www.jstor.org/stable/23864750.

7: Chaldo's Rebellion and Chaldean Resistance (7th Century BCE)

- Finkel, Irving. *The Cyrus Cylinder: The King of Persia's Proclamation from Ancient Babylon.* London: I.B. Tauris, 2018.

8: Chaldean Account of Genesis

- Smith, George. *The Chaldean Account of Genesis,* ed. A. H. Sayce. London: S. Low, Marston, Searle & Rivington, 1880, pp. 3, 10.

- Maspero, Gaston. *History of Egypt, Chaldea, Syria, Babylonia, and Assyria,* Vol. 8, trans. M.L. McClure, ed. A. H. Sayce. London: The Grolier Society, 1903, p. 329.

9: Berossus—The Chaldean Priest of Babylon (3rd Century BCE)

- Encyclopaedia Britannica Editors. "Berosus | Babylonian Historian, Astronomer & Priest." *Britannica.* www.britannica.com/biography/Berosus.

- Attalus. *Eusebius: Chronicle (4) – Translation. Attalus.* www.attalus.org/translate/eusebius4.html.

10: Sibyl, the Chaldean Prophetess (2nd Century BCE)

- Flavius Josephus. *Antiquities of the Jews.* [Bible Study Tools].

- Plutarch. *Life of Alexander.* [Plutarch Alex.pdf].

- *The Sibylline Oracles.* [Bible Hub].

- "Michelangelo's Sistine Chapel: The Sibyls." [Gants Hill URC].

11: Chaldeans Rule in Northern Mesopotamia (7th–6th Century BCE)

- *The Babylonian Chronicles (BM 21901).* Primary cuneiform tablets documenting Babylonian history; the "Fall of Nineveh Chronicle" (ABC 3) records Nabopolassar's capture of Nineveh in 612 BCE, marking Chaldean control over the region. Livius.org.

- Kuhrt, Amélie. *The Ancient Near East, c. 3000–330 BC.* Routledge, 1995.

- Beaulieu, PaulAlain. *The Reign of Nabonidus, King of Babylon 556–539 B.C.* Yale University Press, 1989.

- "The Chaldeans (612–539 BCE)." *Jewish Virtual Library.*

12: Nebuchadnezzar II: The King of Kings (6th Century BCE)

- Weiershäuser and Novotny. *MOCCI Project.* 2015–24. http://oracc.org/ribo/Q005472/.

13: Lives of the Judean Exiles in Babylon (6th Century BCE)

- Pearce, Laurie E., and Cornelia Wunsch. *Documents of Judean Exiles and West Semites in Babylonia in the Collection of David Sofer.* CUSAS Vol. 28, 2014.

- "2,500 Year Old Jewish Babylonian Tablets." *Jewish Virtual Library.* www.jewishvirtuallibrary.org/2-500-year-old-jewish-babylonian-tablets.

- *Interview with Fr. Jose Maniparambil – Scholar and Priest from Kerala, India.* YouTube. youtube.com/live/exJs5w8TzDA.

14: The Chaldeans in Jewish Thought: Talmud and Kabbalah (3rd–13th Century CE)

- *Babylonian Talmud,* Shabbat 156a.
- *The Chaldeans (612–539 BCE). Jewish Virtual Library.* www.jewishvirtuallibrary.org/the-chaldeans-612-539bce.
- *Babylonian Talmud,* Berakhot 55a–56b.
- Matt, Daniel C. *The Zohar: Pritzker Edition.* Stanford University Press, 2004.
- Kaplan, Aryeh. *Sefer Yetzirah: The Book of Creation.* Samuel Weiser Inc., 1990.
- "Relation of the Kabbalah to the Religion of the Chaldeans and Persians." *Sacred Texts Archive.* sacred-texts.com/jud/rph/rph22.htm.
- Blavatsky, Helena P. *The Secret Doctrine.* London: Theosophical Publishing Society, 1888.

15: The Fall of the Chaldean Empire (6th Century BCE)

- Hannona, Habib. *The Chaldean Exodus.* 2022.
- *NeoBabylonian Empire. Wikipedia.* en.wikipedia.org/wiki/Neo-Babylonian_Empire.
- Briant, Pierre. *From Cyrus to Alexander: A History of the Persian Empire.* 2002.

- Kuhrt, Amélie. *The Persian Empire: A Corpus of Sources from the Achaemenid Period.* 2007.

16: The Babylonian Astronomical Diaries (7th–1st Century BCE)

- "The Astronomical Diaries of Babylon." *Discover Historic Jesus.* discoverhistoricjesus.com/babylon-astronomical-diaries/.

- Hunger, Hermann, and Abraham Sachs. *Astronomical Diaries and Related Texts from Babylonia,* Vol. III. Vienna: Austrian Academy of Sciences Press, 1988.

17: Greek Chronicles of the Chaldeans: Anabasis and Beyond (5th–2nd Century BCE)

- Flavius Josephus. *Antiquities of the Jews.* [Bible Study Tools].

- Plutarch. *Life of Alexander.* [Plutarch Alex.pdf].

- *The Sibylline Oracles.* [Bible Hub].

- "Michelangelo's Sistine Chapel: The Sibyls." [Gants Hill URC].

18: Naburimannu, a Chaldean Astronomer and Mathematician (6th–3rd Century BCE)

- Neugebauer, Otto E. *A History of Ancient Mathematical Astronomy,* Part Two IV A 4, 4A (p. 611). Springer, Heidelberg, 1975 (repr. 2004).

- Neugebauer, Otto E. *Astronomical Cuneiform Texts.* 3 vols. London, 1956; 2nd ed. New York: Springer, 1983.

19: Kidinnu, Chaldean Astronomer and Scholar (4th Century BCE)

- Lendering, Jona. "Kidinnu, the Chaldaeans, and Babylonian Astronomy." *Livius.org.* www.livius.org/articles/person/kidinnu-the-chaldaeans-and-babylonian-astronomy/.

- Aaboe, Asger. "Babylonian Mathematics, Astrology and Astronomy." *Cambridge Ancient History,* Vol. 3, Pt. 2, 2nd ed., 1991.

- Hunger, Hermann, and David Pingree. *Astral Sciences in Mesopotamia.* Brill, Leiden, 1999.

20: Sudines, Astronomer and Mathematician (4th Century BCE)

- Strabo. *Geographia* 16.1.6.

- Vettius Valens. *Anthologies* 9.12.

- Pliny the Elder. *Natural History* 37.24.

- *Livius.org.* "Kidinnu, the Chaldaeans, and Babylonian Astronomy." www.livius.org/articles/person/kidinnu-the-chaldaeans-and-babylonian-astronomy/.

21: Seleucus of Seleucia (2nd Century BCE)

- Strabo. *Geographia.*

- Plutarch. *On the Face in the Moon's Orb.*

- "Kidinnu, the Chaldaeans, and Babylonian Astronomy." *Livius.org.* www.livius.org/articles/person/kidinnu-the-chaldaeans-and-babylonian-astronomy/

- Neugebauer, Otto. *The History of Ancient Astronomy.*

22: The Influence of Chaldean Sciences on Greek and Roman Scholars

- *New Catholic Encyclopedia,* 2nd ed. Vol. 10. Washington, D.C.: Catholic University of America Press, 2002, p. 370.

- Flamsteed, John. *Atlas Coelestis.* London: John Crosthwait, 1753. www.davidrumsey.com/luna/servlet/detail/RUMSEY~8~1~365232~90132603

- Collingwood, Cuthbert. "The Astronomy of the Ancient Chaldeans in Relation to the Monuments of Nineveh and Babylon." *Essays on Various Subjects.* 1861, p. 284.

- Greswell, Edward. *Fasti Temporis Catholici,* Vol. II, p. 74.

- Loftus, William Kennett. *Travels and Researches in Chaldaea and Susiana.* London, 1857.

- Strabo. *Geography,* Book XVI, Chap. 1. (LacusCurtius ed.)

- Diodorus Siculus. *Bibliotheca Historica.*

- Pliny the Elder. *Natural History.*

- Josephus, Flavius. *Antiquities of the Jews.*

23: Church of the East (1st Century AD)

- Aprim, Fred. "How Assyrian Found Its Way into the Title of the Church of the East." 2021.

- Goodrich, Samuel G. *A History of All Nations.*

Auburn, N.Y.: Derby & Miller; Cincinnati: H. W. Derby & Co., 1852, p. 55.

24: Julian, the Chaldean (2nd Century CE)

- "Chaldean Oracles." *Wikipedia*. en.wikipedia.org/ wiki/Chaldean_Oracles

- Viglas, Katelis S. "Chaldean and Neo-Platonic Theology." *Philosophia*. philosophia-bg.com/ chaldean-and-neo-platonic-theology

- "Chaldean Oracles." *Hellenic Faith*. hellenicfaith. com/chaldean-oracles

- *Stanford Encyclopedia of Philosophy*. "Iamblichus." plato.stanford.edu/entries/iamblichus

- Majercik, Ruth. *The Chaldean Oracles: Text, Translation and Commentary*. Leiden: Brill, 1989.

- Shaw, Gregory. *Theurgy and the Soul: The Neoplatonism of Iamblichus*. Kettering, OH: Angelico Press, 2014.

25: Chaldeans and Christianity in China (400 AD)

- *The China Review, Or Notes and Queries on the Far East*, Vol. 20 (1885), p. 382.

26: Saint Hirmiz Chaldean Church (397 AD)

- "Mar Hirmiz Keldani Kilisesi: HMML Repository." *Hill Museum & Manuscript Library*. hmml.org/collections/repositories/turkey/ mar-hirmiz-keldani-kilisesi/

- Çetinkaya, Mehmet Yavuz. "Mar Hırmız Keldani Kilisesi." *Türkiye Turizm Ansiklopedisi*.

turkiyeturizmansiklopedisi.com/
mar-hirmiz-keldani-kilisesi

27: Nestorius: The Controversial Archbishop of Constantinople (5th Century AD)

- McGuckin, John Anthony. *The Westminster Handbook to Patristic Theology*. Westminster John Knox Press, 2004.
- Brock, Sebastian P. "Nestorianism." In *The Oxford Dictionary of the Christian Church*. Oxford UP, 2005.
- Meyendorff, John. *Imperial Unity and Christian Divisions: The Church 450–680 AD*. St Vladimir's Seminary Press, 1989.

28: Chaldeans and the Adoption of Nestorianism

- Assemani, Giuseppe Luigi. *De Catholicis Seu Patriarchis Chaldaeorum et Nestorianorum Commentarius*. Rome, 1775.
- Assemanus, Stephanus Evodius & Joseph Simonius Assemanus (eds.). *Bibliotheca Apostolica Vaticana Codicum Manuscriptorum Catalogus,* Pars I, Tomus I. Rome, 1756.
- Bar-Hebraeus. *The Chronography of Gregory Abu'l Faraj*. Oxford: OUP, 1932.
- *Codices Chaldaici sive Syriaci Vaticani Assemaniani*, Vaticanus CCLVIII.
- Badger, George Percy. *The Nestorians and Their Rituals*. London, 1852.

- Assemani, *Bibliotheca orientalis*, IV (1721), p. 75; cited in Joseph, *Modern Assyrians*, p. 6.

29: Discovery of the Chaldean Lost Scrolls

- "PI 00022 – Peshitta Institute – PI Mosul Chaldean Patriarchate 1113." *vHMML Reading Room.* www.vhmml.org/readingRoom/view/502957

- Scher, Addai. "Notice sur les manuscrits syriaques et arabes conservés à l'archevêché chaldéen de Diarbékir." *Journal Asiatique* 10 (1907): 331–62, 385–431.

- *Peshitta Institute. List of Old Testament Peshitta Manuscripts.* Leiden, 1961.

30: Chaldean Christianity in Abbasid Babylonia (9th–10th Century CE)

- Spiegel, Moshe. *History of the Jews: From the Roman Empire to the Early Medieval Period.* New York: Yeshiva University Press, 1956, pp. 328–329, 373.

31: Chonain, the Nestorian Christian (9th Century CE)

- Bar-Hebraeus. *Chronography of Gregory Abu'l Faraj.* Oxford: OUP, 1932.

- Assemani, Giuseppe Luigi. *De Catholicis Seu Patriarchis Chaldaeorum et Nestorianorum Commentarius.* Rome, 1775.

- Badger, George Percy. *The Nestorians and Their Rituals.* London, 1852.

32: Ibn Wahshiyyah: A 10th-Century Muslim Scientist, Alchemist, Translator

- Hämeen-Anttila, Jaakko. *The Last Pagans of Iraq: Ibn Wahshiyya and His Nabatean Agriculture.* Leiden: Brill, 2006, p. 16.

- Müller, Max. *Lectures on the Science of Language.* London: Longman, 1861, p. 233.

- Yale University. "Echoes of Egypt: The Treatise of the 93 Alphabets."

33: Early Medieval Christian Rule (10th–11th Century CE)

- Richard, Jean. *The Crusades c. 1071–c. 1291.* Cambridge University Press, 1999, p. 22.

34: Michael the Great (1199)

- Michael the Syrian. *Chronicle of Michael the Great, Patriarch of the Syrians.* Trans. Robert Bedrosian. 1870 ed.

- Josephus, Flavius. *Antiquities of the Jews,* Book I, Chs. 6–7.

35: Sabrisho ibn alMasihi (1226–1256 AD)

- "Chaldeans." *Encyclopedia.com.* www.encyclopedia.com/humanities/encyclopedias-almanacs-transcripts-and-maps/chaldeans

- "Chaldean Christians." *Catholic Encyclopedia. New Advent.*

- "Sabrisho V." *Wikipedia.*

36: Chaldeans in Medieval Pisa (12th–13th Century AD)

- Hutton, Edward. *Florence and Northern Tuscany with Genoa.* New York, 1907, p. 85.

37: Yahballaha III (1281–1317 AD)

- "Yahballaha III." *Wikipedia.*
- "Chaldean Christians." *Catholic Encyclopedia. New Advent.*

38: *The Little Book on the Knowledge of the World* and the Chaldeans in Mesopotamia (14th-15th Century)

- Giovanni (John), Dominican friar and Archbishop of Sulthanyeh. *Libellus de Notitia Orbis* (1404). Ed. Anton Kern, in *Archivum Fratrum Praedicatorum*, Vol. 8 (1938), p. 100. Available online: *Libellus de Notitia Orbis (Anton Kern ed., 1938).*

39: 1457 World Map

- Fra Mauro. *Mappa Mundi* (ca. 1457). *Fra Mauro World Map*, Venice, Biblioteca Nazionale Marciana, ms. It. IV, 90 = 5584, detail showing "Babylonia (Caldea)." Retrieved from Chaldean Heritage Foundation

40: The Legacy and Marginalization of the Chaldeans

- HämeenAnttila, Jaakko. *The Last Pagans of Iraq: Ibn Wahshiyya and His Nabatean Agriculture.* Leiden: Brill, 2006.
- AlMasʿudi, Ali ibn alHusayn. *Kitāb alTanbīh wa al-Ishrāf.* Ed. M.J. de Goeje. Leiden: Brill, 1894.
- AlSuyuti, Jalal alDin Abd alRahman ibn Abi Bakr.

AlMuzhir fi Ulum alLughah wa Anwa'iha. Bulaq: al-Matba'ah alKubra alSaniyah, 1865.

- Maimonides, Moses. *The Guide for the Perplexed.* Trans. Michael Friedländer. London: George Routledge & Sons, 1904.

41: Persecution and the Loss of Chaldean Heritage

- Shikwana, Yousif. *2000 Years of Massacres.* Trans. Mahir Awrahem, March 7, 2023.

42: The 1445 Cyprus Union with the Vatican

- "Catholic Encyclopedia: Chaldean Christians." *New Advent.* www.newadvent.org/cathen/03559a.htm

43: Patriarchate of Yohannan Sulaqa (1551)

- "Catholic Encyclopedia: Chaldean Christians." *New Advent.* www.newadvent.org/cathen/03559a.htm

- Assemani, Giuseppe Luigi. *HistoricalChronological Commentary on the Catholic or Patriarchs of the Chaldeans and Nestorians.*

44: Pietro della Valle and Sitti Maani (17th Century)

- Della Valle, Pietro. *Viaggi di Pietro Della Valle il Pellegrino.*

- Della Valle, Pietro. *Funerale della Signora Sitti Maani Gioerida della Valle.* Rome, 1627.

- "Della Valle, Pietro." *Encyclopaedia Iranica.* www.iranicaonline.org/articles/della-valle/

45: Nation of the Chaldeans (1617)

- Anonymous. *De Chaldaeorum Natione, ejusque Patriarcha.* Rome: Typographia Sacrae

Congregationis de Propaganda Fide, 1617. [Vatican Library, Vat. Lat. 6432 ff. 112–115.]

46: The Scribes and Writers of Chaldean Heritage

- Zadok, Ran. "The Scribes of Borsippa in the First Millennium BC: A Preliminary Survey."

47: Josephus Adjutus, Chaldean Scholar (17th Century)

- Henny, Sundar. "Nathanael of Leukas and the Hottinger Circle: The Wanderings of a SeventeenthCentury Greek Archbishop." *International Journal of the Classical Tradition* 27 (3), 2020, p. 453.

- Brentjes, Burchard. "Josephus Adjutus, der Chaldäer zu Wittenberg." *Wissenschaftliche Zeitschrift der MartinLutherUniversität HalleWittenberg: Gesellschafts und Sprachwissenschaftliche Reihe* 26 (1977): 131–38.

48: Elias alMusili: First Middle Easterner to Travel to the Americas (17th Century)

- Ghobrial, JohnPaul A. *The Secret Life of Elias of Babylon and the Uses of Global Microhistory.* Beth Mardutho: The Syriac Institute, 2014.

- Farah, Caesar E. *An Arab's Journey to Colonial Spanish America: The Travels of Elias alMûsili in the Seventeenth Century.* 2003.

- Rabbath, Antoine. *AlMashriq,* 1905–1906.

- Namou, Weam. *Elias alMusili: A Chaldean Priest's Journey to the New World in the 1600s.*

49: Alqosh—A Chaldean Town and the Tomb of the Prophet Nahumm

- Fraser, James Baillie. *Mesopotamia and Assyria, from the Earliest Ages to the Present Time; with Illustrations of Their Natural History.* London: Oliver & Boyd, 1842, p. 59.

50: Maria Theresa Asmar: Author and Traveler (19th Century)

- Asmar, Maria Theresa. *Memoirs of a Babylonian Princess.* 1844.

- Namou, Weam. *Maria Theresa Asmar: A Chaldean Woman's Story During the 1800s.*

51: Hormuzd Rassam: A Pioneer in Mesopotamian Archaeology

- Ainsworth, William Francis. *Travels and Researches in Asia Minor, Mesopotamia, Chaldea, and Armenia,* Vol. I. London: John W. Parker, 1842.

- Rassam, Hormuzd. *Asshur and the Land of Nimrod.* London: Curts & Jennings, 1897.

- Hanoosh, Yasmeen. *The Chaldeans: Politics and Identity in Iraq and the American Diaspora.* Ann Arbor: University of Michigan Press, 2019, p. 31.

- Layard, Austen Henry. *Nineveh and Its Remains.* London: John Murray, 1849.

- Robson, Eleanor. *Ancient Knowledge Networks: A Social Geography of Cuneiform Scholarship in FirstMillennium Assyria and Babylonia.* London: UCL Press, 2019.

- Goodhart, George. "Unburying an Archaeologist: The Forgotten Story of Hormuzd Rassam." *Uncomfortable Oxford,* 30 Nov 2023. www.un-comfortableoxford.com/unburying-an-archaeolo-gist-the-forgotten-story-of-hormuzd-rassam

- Rassam, A. Hormuzd. *British Policy in Assyrian Settlement.* Letter to the British Foreign Office. British Library archives.

52: Rev. Joseph Naayem: Priest, Scholar, and Humanitarian (1868 – 1964)

- Naayem, Rev. Joseph. *Shall This Nation Die?* London: J. M. Dent & Sons, 1920.

- Namou, Weam. *Joseph Naayem: A Chaldean Priest's Story During the 1915 Genocide,* Hermiz Publishing, 2021.

53: The Modern Assyrian Identity

- Xenophon. *Anabasis.*

- Joseph, John. *The Modern Assyrians of the Middle East: Encounters with Western Christian Missions, Archeologists & Colonial Powers.*

- Wigram, W. A. *Our Smallest Ally.*

- Ainsworth, W. E. *Travels and Researches in Asia Minor, Mesopotamia, Chaldea, and Armenia.*

54: Evidence of the Chaldean Presence in Modern and Historical Contexts

- *Iraq Constitution,* Article 125. http://www.iraqde-mocracyproject.org

- *The Annals of the Propaganda of Faith,* Dominican Fathers, 1750.
- *Iraqi Census of 1957,* Kirkuk Brigade data.
- Google Search on Baghdad churches, July 2025.

55: The Chaldean Language: A Legacy of Aramaic

- Hanoosh, Yasmeen. *The Chaldeans: Politics and Identity in Iraq and the American Diaspora.* I.B. Tauris, 2019.
- *The Book of the Sacred Magic of AbraMelin the Mage,* trans. S. L. MacGregor Mathers. 1932.
- Mar Touma Odu. *Chaldean Language Dictionary.* 1897.
- *Θεολογούμενα Παντοδαπά. Sive de Natura, Ortu, Progressu, et Studio Veræ Theologiæ Libri Sex.* Oxford: Hen. Hall, 1661, p. 311.
- *Vernacular Bible Explorer.* "Spontaneous Translation." 2025. vernacularbibleexplorer.substack.com/p/spontaneous-translation
- *Cambridge Chronicle and University Journal,* Oct 15, 1830.
- Brock, Sebastian P. *An Introduction to Syriac Studies.* 1980.
- Assemani, Stephanus Evodius. *Bibliothecae Apostolicae Vaticanae.* 1756. archive.org/stream/assemani-bav-manus-1/Assemani-BAV%20Manus-1_djvu.txt
- Gessford, Roy. *Preserving the Chaldean Aramaic Language.* Let in the Light Publishing, 2020, p. 3.

56: DNA Testing

- Reich, David. *Who We Are and How We Got Here: Ancient DNA and the New Science of the Human Past.* 2018.

- Jobling, M. A., Hollox, E., Hurles, M., Kivisild, T., & TylerSmith, C. *Human Evolutionary Genetics: Origins, Peoples, and Disease.* 2nd ed., 2013.

- Marcus, J. H., and C. Posth. "Ancient DNA and the Study of Human History." *Nature* 551 (7681), 2017, pp. 549–558.

- International Society of Genetic Genealogy (ISOGG). *ISOGG Wiki: DNA and Ethnicity Testing.* isogg.org/wiki

- Bardill, J., Bader, A. C., Garrison, N. A., et al. "Advancing the Ethics of Paleogenomics." *Science* 360 (6387), 2018, pp. 384–385.

57: The Thrones and Palaces of Babylon and Nineveh (1876)

- Newman, John Philip. *The Thrones and Palaces of Babylon and Nineveh.* New York: Harper & Brothers, 1876.

- Jammo, Mar Sarhad Youssab, Ph.D. "Chaldean Identity in Historical Documents." *Chaldean Nation.* chaldeannation.com/chaldean-identity-1/

58: Chaldeans in Argentina

- Namou, Weam. "The Lost Tribe." *Chaldean News,* March 1, 2023. www.chaldeannews.com/2023-content/2023/3/1/the-lost-tribe

59: Chaldeans in India

- Namou, Weam. "Chaldean Catholics in India." *Chaldean News,* Jan 5, 2023. www.chaldeannews.com/2023-content/2023/1/5/chaldean-catholics-in-india

- *Corrected Missal of the Chaldeans or Nestorians of Malabar,* Codices Syriaci (Assemanian Library, Vatican). Cataloged in Joseph Simonius Assemani, *Bibliotheca Orientalis,* 1719–1728.

- *Gopiges Chaldaigi sive Syriaci Vaticani Assemaniani.*

60: Iraqi Muslim Chaldeans

- Namou, Weam. "From Discovery to Legacy." *Chaldean News,* June 30, 2025. www.chaldeannews.com/2025-content/2025/6/30/from-discovery-to-legacy

61: Chaldean Woman in Afghanistan

- Turabaz, Sheila. "From the Nineveh Plains to Kabul." *Chaldean News,* Aug 30, 2025. www.chaldeannews.com/2025-content/2025/8/30/from-the-nineveh-plains-to-kabul

IMAGE AND ILLUSTRATION REFERENCES

Introduction

@ant_____. "Screenshot of Wikipedia edit history showing revisions to Tel Keppe population description." Posted 23 October 2023 on *X* (formerly Twitter). Available at x.com/ant_____/status/1874018142235877864.

Entry 1. Who Are the Chaldeans?

Gerhard Mercator and Iodocus Hondius, *Paradisus* (Amsterdam: Ioannes Janssonius, 1607). www.davidrumsey.com/luna/servlet/detail/RUMSEY~8~1~283496~90055907:Paradisus#.

Entry 2. Abraham's Lineage and the Chaldeans

Library of Congress Prints and Photographs Division. Digital ID matpc 16096 / LC DIG matpc 16096 (digital file from original). Washington, D.C., U.S.A.

Entry 4. First Mention in Archaeology (9th Century BCE)

"Ur of the Chaldees (Ur Kaśdim): A Historical and Archaeological Narrative." *Wikipedia.*

Entry 5. The Chaldean Tribes and the Nimrud Letters (9th–7th Century BCE)

Abdullah Frères, *Constantinople — Chaldean,* photograph, 1869. Library of Congress Prints and Photographs Division, Washington, D.C.

Entry 8. Chaldean Account of Genesis

George Smith (1840–1876), biographical portrait, Assyriology archives.

Entry 9. Berossus — The Chaldean Priest of Babylon (3rd Century BCE)

Berossus Caldaeus.

Entry 23. Church of the East (1st Century AD)

Humble Shimun, Patriarch of the Chaldeans. Seal used for official letters until 1976.

Entry 26. Saint Hirmiz Chaldean Church (397 AD)

Saint Hirmiz Chaldean Church – 4th Century – Mardin – Turkey, photograph.

Entry 28. The Chaldeans and the Adoption of Nestorianism

Bain News Service, *Nestorian (Assyrian) Christian Family Making Butter, Mawana, Persia,* photograph, ca. early 20th century. Library of Congress, Prints and Photographs Division, Washington, D.C. Reproduction No. LC DN 20146 (BAIN) [LCN2014683072]. Accessed at www.loc.gov/item/2014683072/.

Entry 39. 1457 Map of the World

Fra Mauro, *Mappa Mundi* (ca. 1457). Fra Mauro World Map, Venice, Biblioteca Nazionale Marciana, ms. It. IV, 90 = 5584, detail showing "Babylonia (Caldea)." Chaldean Heritage Foundation Collection.

Entry 44. Pietro della Valle and Sitti Maani (17th Century)

(1) *Sitti Maani Gioerida della Valle.*

(2) *Pietro della Valle.* Portraits from *Funerale della Signora Sitti Maani Gioerida della Valle* (1627).

Entry 46. The Scribes and Writers of Chaldean Heritage

Chaldean Catholic Bookbinders in Mosul, photograph, 1890.

Entry 47. Josephus Adjutus (17th Century Chaldean Scholar)

Portrait of Josephus Adjutus, aged 40 (1647).

Entry 49. Alqosh—A Chaldean Town and the Tomb of the Prophet Nahum

Qasha Oraha Shikwana and his Son Ishaq, photograph by the Saffarian Brothers, Mosul, 1890. GetArchive.net, boudewijnhuijgens.getarchive.net/media/qasha-oraha-shikwana-and-his-son-ishaq-e4c550.

Entry 50. Maria Theresa Asmar: Author and Traveler (19th Century)

Memoirs of a Babylonian Princess frontispiece (1844).

Entry 51. Hormuzd Rassam: A Pioneer in Mesopotamian Archaeology

Mr. Hormuzd Rassam vide Layard's Nineveh, portrait study of Hormuzd Rassam (1854).

Entry 52. Rev. Joseph Naayem: Priest, Scholar, and Humanitarian (1868 – 1964)

Rev. Joseph Naayem, dressed as a Bedouin as he escapes the genocide.

Entry 53. The Modern Assyrian Identity

Newspaper article, "Nestorians, of Chaldean Race," *Democrat and Chronicle* (Rochester, NY), August 20, 1905.

Entry 57. The Thrones and Palaces of Babylon and Nineveh (1876)

Chaldean Catholics in Mardin, 1904, originally published in *Album de la Mission Française (Capucins)* (1904), edited by Fr. Raphaël, a Capuchin friar; later reprinted in *Arménie: Il y a mille ans, Ani,* and available through the Virtual Genocide Memorial archive, which documents photographic sources related to Christian minorities in the Ottoman Empire.

Epilogue

Figure 1. Charles West, *A Chaldean Lady* (1782), crayon drawing. Published by John Boydell. Collection of the National Gallery of Denmark (*Statens Museum for Kunst*).

Figure 2. Wenceslaus Hollar, *Chaldean Man,* from the title page of *Decapla in Psalmos* (1639). Etching depicting ten male busts representing different nationalities: a Syrian, Hebrew, Arab, Chaldean, Egyptian, Greek, Ancient Roman, Gaul, Spaniard, and Modern Roman. Collection of *The Metropolitan Museum of Art,* New York.